MOVE OVER!

Humorous Stories and Verses

Vera M Murray

Copyright © Vera M Murray. 2013, 2019

All rights reserved. No part of this publication may be reproduced, stored in a retrieval system, or transmitted in any form or by any means without the prior written permission of the copyright owner, through the publisher, nor be otherwise circulated in any form of binding or cover other than that in which it is published and without a similar condition being imposed on the subsequent purchaser.

All characters, events, and places recorded in this publication are fictitious and any resemblance to real persons, living or dead, is purely coincidental.

Assisted by Bent Banana Books, 24 Lorraine Court, Lawnton, Queensland, Australia 4501.

A CIP Catalogue record for this book is available from the Australian National Library, Canberra.

ISBN NO: 978-0-9805684-9-3 (paperback)

AUTHOR: Vera (Veronica) M Murray, 4 Leis Parade, Lawnton, Queensland, 4501, Australia ....2013.

Cover Design by Ken Armstrong, Albany Creek, Qld.

DEDICATION

I dedicate this book to my children,
Joanne Croyden, Frank Fisk, and their families.

My thanks go to Bernie Dowling, Anne Olsson and
Roslyn Rawlinson, for help with editing.

The author, Vera Murray's previous full length books:

MOVE OVER JAMES BOND AND OTHER STORIES was published in 2009 under Vera Mary Murray.

Some of the stories in this book are inspired by some personal experience, or the experiences of others who at various times have crossed the writer's path, with however exceptions. Some stories are serious, some humorous and cover a wide area of life, while others are for light enjoyable reading, i.e. a Trip to Mars, meeting possible Aliens, Love is Like the Measles, A Bloke Can be Real Unlucky, and many others.

Three of the stories were revised for entry in 'Move Over! Humorous Stories and Verses.

* * * * * * * *

LEAP YEAR BLOOD LUST was published under Vera M. Murray in 2011.

It is the story of the ruthless Lord of the Manor's hold over the local townspeople who live in the eerie village of Rockville, situated on the edge of the ocean. A leap-year ancient curse is brought to life when a member of the Allen family is drawn into the town always on February 29thg in each leap year. What happens to Greg Allen and the town's people in the leap year of 2004 is chilling.

Inspired by a visit to Tasmania's South and West Coast where the slag heaps of abandoned mines are to be found, the setting for this story was set there.

CONTENTS

Granddad's Teeth (poem)	7
No Flies on Me (poem)	8
MOVE OVER! Assignment 1	10
Birthday Gift for My Wife	21
Getting the Sack (poem)	21
Doodling at the Office Desk (poem)	22
2 a.m. In the bar (poem)	24
MOVE OVER! Assignment 2	24
I Hate Being Late (poem)	38
My Own Worst Enemy (poem)	40
MOVE OVER! Assignment 3	42
Life's Journey (poem)	53
A Bathroom Crisis (poem)	56
MOVE OVER! Assignment 4	58
Dave on His Ma-In-Law (poem)	74
Retirement Dream (poem)	75
MOVE OVER! Assignment 5	77
The Battle of the Bulge (poem)	88
Senior Ladies' Health Walk (poem)	91
MOVE OVER! Assignment 6	93
Waiting for the Postman (poem)	109
When You're Over the Hill (poem)	110
MOVE OVER! Assignment 7	112
A Writers' Meeting (poem)	130
The Pin Tin (poem)	132
Hanna's Ghost (poem)	134

GRANDDAD'S TEETH

Granddad hunched and clutched his knees,
As the mighty sneeze exploded.
His teeth flew out his open mouth,
As if his head was loaded.

It spread his germs throughout the house,
To each ceiling, through each door.
All the family tried to hide,
From a flu they can't ignore.

Through his double yellow gums,
Granddad swore, Granddad spluttered,
"Where's me teeth? Where have they gone?"
"The grandkid took 'em." He then uttered.

Granddad didn't have a clue,
That the family dog had carried 'em,
Down behind the outside loo,
And there it was he buried 'em.

'Go, get a new set,' we all said,
But he's too tight-fisted, you see.
So now we feed him soup and sops,
While we all feast on fruit and chops.

NO FLIES ON ME

He acted so smart.
It was quite a lark,
When he came to work,
On a sheep station,
Backa Bourke.

'No flies on me,' he said,
As he wheeled the lead,
Never listenin' to the boss,
'Cos, according to him,
He already knew the lot.

'No flies on me,' he said,
But when the sheep saw him,
They all stood still and stared.
'When I'm the foreman I'll fix you,'
He spat and cursed at them.

'No flies on me,' he said,
'This shearin's a breeze,'
As he pocketed the shears.
'At dodging work I'm an expert,'
At that I have the expertise.'

'No flies on me,' he said.
'I'll woo the boss' daughter,
Though she's loose-lipped like a cow.
Then I'll own this place,
Soon as her dad's dead.'

'No flies on me,' he said.
'I'm gunna tell the boss I'll wed,
His ten-ton daughter Septisenia.
He'll be so pleased to be rid of Septi,
He'll make me foreman on the spot.

'No flies on me,' he said,
With so much confidence,
The other workers fell,
Laughin' behind his back,
While waiting for the fall.

'No flies on me,' he said,
When a new owner took over.
But this one was 'clued' up.
He checked 'no flies' out,
Then gave 'no flies' the sack.

'No flies on HIM,' we said,
When 'No flies' got the boot.
So at the farewell for the silly coot,
We shouted, 'NO FLIES ON HIM,
ONLY THE SPOTS WHERE THEY'VE BEEN.'

* * * * * * * *

CROSS-EYED CONVERSATION

What did one eye say to the other? "Don't look now, but something between us smells."

MOVE OVER! Assignment 1
A Friend's Deceit

WHEN the balaclava-clad man came running from the chemist shop it was the legs that betrayed the robber as his ankles became exposed as he raced away. Nardia had seen them before at very close quarters. A distinct 'x'-shaped scar was on the outside of one ankle. Miles had told her he had fallen off a cliff when he was a child. Nardia doubted that, and the thought that a previous lover had scarred him had surfaced in her mind, but why on the ankle? The recall died as she bent almost double to be concealed behind a parked car as his sandals, clapping on the concrete path, came closer. The sound lessened as he ran past. Peering out, she saw him make a long stride over the wide gutter, then disappear around the corner. Two men were chasing him but he was too fast. They returned, shaking their heads with disappointment.

Nardia debated with herself as to what she should do...perhaps report her suspicions to the police who had now arrived. *No. There must be some mistake.* Her thoughts tumbled over one another. *Maybe it wasn't him. I only had a glance. Perhaps it was only dirty marks that formed a similar pattern.*

Nardia shrugged and went on to finish her shopping. However, still plagued with worry at the possibility of it being Miles, she began to regret leaving a duplicate key to her front door hidden in her letterbox. It was Miles' idea. He told her he was prone to losing small things like keys. It was a failing of his, he had said. She thought it unusual, but as he wanted it that way she agreed to it. *When I see him I'll demand to know where he was today, whether he gets offended or not.*

On arriving home, laden down with her purchases, she slipped her key into the lock on the front door. Quickly pushing the door open with her shoulder she bundled herself and her purchases inside. Straightening up once inside, she reeled in shock. A complete stranger was sitting in her lounge chair, and smiling at her.

"Who...?"

"Relax, I'm Warren's friend Doug. He said to meet him here. I was to wait outside, but I found the key...not very well hidden...so made myself comfortable. I hope you don't mind."

"How dare you! And for your information there's no Warren here. Leave before I call the police."

He ignored her. "Has your flat-mate, Miles got an 'x' scar on his leg?"

Nardia nodded.

"What's he call himself now... Miles, Des? no matter. He said he'd have something for me and I'm not leaving 'til I get it." He levelled his gaze at her and slowly patted his pocket.

Nardia decided that was a hint he had a gun and backed away.

"Don't worry. I won't be staying once your Miles gets here. Look lady, I've got no beef with you, but I don't want you to cause any trouble for us. Look, make some coffee, relax, and in no time we'll be gone." She had a strong urge to object, but decided it might be safer not to.

She turned to enter the kitchen and he rose to follow her, but before she could move forward he asked, "Where'd you meet Warren/Miles?"

"College," she replied.

"Ah...selling drugs to the students...smart move."

"Drugs! Never!"

"I see he's kept it from you. Smooth lad is your Miles. Safe as houses cottoning on to someone clean like you, but he's into drugs, and I'm here to collect what he owes his supplier."

The sound of the front door opening made them both turn. In the doorway stood Miles. He first greeted the visitor. "G'day mate...knew you'd be here." He then walked over to Nardia and quickly kissed her on the cheek. She was shocked at his audacity. Before she could make a quick retort, he was walking towards the main bedroom. Nardia was about to follow him but he waved her back. She remained standing, nervous and frightened.

He reappeared, weighted down by his belongings. Doug relieved him of his suitcase, and the two men prepared to leave. The stranger reached the door first, while Miles slipped an arm around Nardia who squirmed away. She was fearful they would make her go with them, but Miles dropped his arm and smiled his boyish grin.

"It was nice Nardia...never forget you. Maybe we can get together again when I'm in town."

"If you ever come within a mile of me I'll call the police and tell them you're a drug dealer."

He laughed. It was a laugh Nardia had loved for its happy sound. "And what will you tell them my sweet? You have no proof I have anything to do with drugs so who would believe you? No one knows I've been staying here with you so I can say I've never met you. "Bye sweetheart...till next time I see you." He followed Doug out, through the front door. Nardia quickly bolted it behind them.

Shaking, she went to the window to be sure they had actually left. Miles saw her. He smiled and waved. In his hand were the keys of a car. She knew he did not own one and she had not seen any car out front when she had returned home, but now there was one parked there. *Perhaps that's stolen too.*

Worried she might find traces of drugs in her flat, Nardia checked the house, but the only reminder of Miles was a statue he had brought her on her birthday. It was positioned on the top of the television set. 'That's going out tomorrow,' she decided.

What if he comes back? She checked to make sure all windows and access doors were securely locked. Knowing Miles still had a key she pushed the heaviest lounge chair against the locked front door.

She sank down into the closest chair knowing that any story she told would have a ring of a disgruntled thrown-away lover to it. *I've been tricked but what can I do? I have to do something, but what?* She knew she would have to prove he actually existed. He always said he was too busy studying when she wanted him to go with her to meet her friends. Now she realised it was part of his guise.

That night she slept spasmodically. At 6 am she decided she could not remain alone and scared. *There's no way I'm going to leave the place today, but I need some advice, and company.* After 9 am that morning she 'phoned her workplace, advising them she would not be in that day. She then called her girlfriend Meta. On hearing Nardia's urgent request, Meta immediately promised to be there as soon as she could.

Half an hour later, seated together on the lounge Nardia had pulled away from the front door, Meta was comforting Nardia as she related the whole series of events. "He told me his ex-wife was after him for half his bank account and their house, none of which she was entitled to. He said she kept hassling him through a solicitor, so he had to keep out of sight. He made me promise I wouldn't tell anyone he was living with me. I believed him. How dumb can you be?"

"We all make mistakes Nardia, but drugs? That's bad. You could have been involved. You're lucky he left."

"But he might come back," was the nervous response.

"True, so you must tell the police. They'll keep an eye on the place I'm sure." Meta rose. "I'll make some coffee."

As she passed the TV she remarked. "What happened to that photo you had on the small table...the one of you with your favourite uncle?"

"I don't know...I must have put it somewhere else. I can't remember."

"You looked lovely in that photo. Maybe Miles took it for a keepsake."

This made Nardia smile. "That's the joke of the week. He didn't like me. He used me."

"So we have to make sure he doesn't come back. You must tell the police."

Nardia, knowing she had no choice if she were to feel safe, agreed.

....

At the Drug Squad's headquarters the CEO, Mr Grant Stand, called Ernest Moneylove, worshipper and devotee of that famous spy, James Bond, into his office. Ernest Moneylove had changed his name from Elfie Jones so it was more in line with those in James Bond movies. He so admired James Bond that he did everything he could to act like that successful solver of crime and charming lady swooner. Ernest's narrow, bony build and short height, plus his plain features and largish lips, appeared to be against him, especially in the beautiful girl area. Ernest thought otherwise. Now, as a member of the Government's Drug Squad, he held the belief that, in his fight against illegal drugs, he would eventually stand at the top beside James Bond, or better still make him move over.

After many attempts, he had obtained a transfer from his position as head office clerk in the Transport Department to the Drug Squad. The Chief of the drug squad, Grant Stand, after reading Ernest's vague reference, failed to stop the transfer, so he was not in the mood to treat Moneylove on the same level as his favourite agent, John Smith. As Smith was on another assignment he was left with no option but to involve this new member. He sighed before he spoke.

"We've had a report that a drug dealer we're looking for, a Desmond... Miles...Warren, or whatever he calls himself, has finally been traced. He's an expert in hiding his identity, which has made him impossible to catch so far. This time we're in luck. He's been staying with a Nardia Barlow. Here are some photos of her."

Ernest studied them carefully and handed it back. *She's quite a James Bond beauty.* He reluctantly handed the photos back into the Chief's hand.

His boss continued. "She thinks her Miles, who is definitely our man, as she tells us he has a scar on his ankle that has been mentioned in other reports, may come back again. Although I think it's mighty unlikely, at least for a while, I'm assigning you to watch her house. If any young man appears on her property, call on the police back-up to have him arrested. If you succeed in nabbing this criminal it will be a 'feather in your cap,' so to speak. 'I have my doubts on that score," he muttered softly to himself.

"Thank you SIR," was Ernest's enthusiastic response while straightening up and pushing out his flat chest. *It's not a James Bond type of job, except for the beautiful girl involved, but it's on the way up, so get ready to move aside James.*

His boss ignored Ernest to continue. "The house was checked and some white power was found inside a rather large carved statue he had given Nardia. It had been hollowed out and also contained a large number of $100 notes. We believe he'll come back to collect it, though I'm sure he'll lie low for a few weeks at least. He wouldn't be stupid enough to show up during the day, so we have to be ready for after dark. I know it's a menial job but you are the one best suited for it."

James Bond never turned down a job. With success, I'll be able to establish a good reputation, even though I'm new in the job. John Smith has already shown a superior attitude towards me, and my fellow workers informed me he takes every opportunity to take credit for others' work, so I can't trust him. I'm glad he's on some other job and well away from me. At the thought Ernest narrowed his eyes, jutted out his chin as he has seen James Bond do in his films, and said. "Thank you Sir."

His boss sighed. "You are to cruise past her home several times a day, and sit in the car near the big tree outside from dusk onward. Grab anyone...you'll have backup...who comes within proximity of the house, and is acting even slightly suspiciously. Success in this job will help you a little bit up the ladder, so follow instructions to a 't'."

"I will SIR."

Several days later Ernest, on guard duty outside Nardia's residence, was settled comfortably behind the steering wheel of the office car. As the sun had set and it was becoming too dark to continue reading, Ernest put down his book of spy stories. He was beginning to feel his stomach groaning, and decided to satisfy his hunger.

About to start the car to drive to the nearest 'takeaway' food outlet, the upper part of a man's body blacked out the side window. A knock came on the window beside Ernest. Squinting, he found himself looking at the face of an elderly man with a thick white beard. He wound down the window, and asked, "How can I help you?"

The man spoke slowly and coughed almost constantly. "Sorry to trouble you mister. Are you parked outside No 3, Nardia's house? My sight's bad, so I can't read numbers, especially when it's so dark. I'm Nardia's uncle and I have a present I promised her. It's a lovely photo of both of us. I had it enlarged and framed for her" He ripped the paper from the packet he was holding. He held it up for Ernest, who switched on the overhead light, to see it closely. "That's Nardia and that's me," he explained, unnecessarily.

Ernest nodded. He noted the likeness to the man in several of Nardia's snapshots he had seen at headquarters, who Nardia had told them was her uncle. He decided these were definitely Nardia and the man in those prints. He handed it back. As the man rewrapped it he added."She's my favourite niece. I'll go and give it to her. She's going to love it."

"I suppose she might." A now disinterested Moneylove half-heartedly muttered.

The man waddled off and Ernest watched him reach the front door and heard it open.

Ernest checked his watch, then drove to pull in at the closest food take-away outlet.

....

"Hello Nardia."

Move Over

Nardia, settling some magazines in the lounge, swung around puzzled when the door opened. It had been locked. The man now facing her would pass for her uncle, but she recognised the voice. It was Miles. She thought of screaming but knew that if he became violent it would be too late for the guard to reach her in time. She decided her only course was to try to bluff him.

"I can see how you fooled the police, but I'm going to scream if you don't leave NOW." With her heart pounding she willed it to be a success.

"That guard of yours won't hear you. He's gone for his dinner. Always does at this time every night. All I want is that statue I gave you, and you won't hear from me again."

Nardia knew she had failed.

Suddenly the door flung open and in rushed two policemen with guns pointed at Miles. A man wearing a drug squad badge that Marcia did not recognise, accompanied them.

Miles, with a look of utter disbelief, did not move as they arrested and handcuffed him. As they were marching him to the door he turned back to Nardia. "Nice knowing you sweetheart...bye 'till next time." Before she could say 'dream on,' they had gone. Nardia sank down into the lounge chair and burst into tears of relief.

When Ernest returned to his car, holding a large hamburger, he was astounded to see 'pushy' Smithy, the fellow drug officer determined to rise to the top with the least effort. He was marching out of Nardia's property with two policemen who were holding on to the man Ernest believed was Nardia's uncle.

When he was told by the leading officer that this was the drug courier they were after, Ernest thought, *'Fancy it being her uncle. I thought the dealer would be much younger. Even James Bond would've had difficulty with this one.'*

John Smith wore a satisfied grin on his face as he reached Ernest. He stopped to add."The Boss thought I should check on how you were doing. Lucky I did. Nardia won't be troubled with this bloke again after we've dealt with him." As they reached the newly arrived police van, Smith turned again to Ernest. "This will go good on my record .... shame you missed out."

Moneylove wanted to kick him in the shins, but instead he comforted himself with the thought, *James had his set-backs too, but he made up for it on his next assignment, and that's what I'll be doing. Just you wait Smithy.*

BIRTHDAY GIFT FROM A WIFE

Dear husband, you're kept busy
By me and your work boss.
But now it's your birthday
I wish you one great day,
And grant you your greatest wish,
To indulge in your native laziness,
And dream at will, and, in that daze,
Solve all the problems of the world,
From a horizontal position,
As you always said you could.

GETTING THE SACK

The day I go,
Is the day I'm sacked,
And I go with woe,
Because I've been packed

DOODLING AT THE OFFICE DESK

These few verses,
'bout nothing at all,
Were created by me,
'Cos I can't be seen idle.

With moments to fill,
I don't delay.
I pick up pen or pencil,
And doodle the time away.

With many long strokes,
And delicate hand movements,
Plus lots of dots and scribbles,
I have pictures momentous.

With oodles of doodles,
To my great credit,
There is no doubt,
I'm a jolly great artist.

The office 'psychologist',
Now tells me...my doodles,
I mean, those that he's read,
Form patterns most revealing.

'Poor thing's a basket case,'
He told the whole staff.
'Just look at that scroll,
It shows tendencies suicidal.'

'No, no!' I scream, disgusted.
'You know, that's being unjust.

Move Over

I'm so bright, you once said,
And extremely well adjusted.'

I snatch my doodles back.
'They've been tampered with,
By someone who needs the sack,
Who's stole and altered them.'

When the giggling office boy,
Admitted that, behind my back,
He pinched and rewrote them,
The mystery ended there and then.

They'll now be locked away,
Behind a key each day,
Away from all…but me,
'Cos rare treasures they be.

2 A.M. IN THE BAR

Danger lurks here.
Danger...here?
Yes, my friend!
What danger?
You can't see it?
No, I can't.

It lurks nearby.
In this bar?
Yes, be careful.
Of what, tell me.
Her roving eyes.
On me, where?

Yes, move, move.
Why should I?
She's too close.
Hello, pretty eyes.
Take care, my friend.
I will, I always do.

This time you're not.
Pretty eyes...so close.
You've been warned.
Of eyes, ha! ha!
Move away...now.
Pretty eyes want kiss?

Too late, too late.
Pretty eyes gone!
You'll need a drink.
Where's me wallet?
I warned you.
Oh...Mother!

MOVE OVER!   Assignment 2 Narrow Escape

AT the Drug Squad office, Ernest Moneylove once again stood fronting Mr Grant Stand's desk.

"I have an assignment for you Moneylove," announced the Chief. Ernest was puffed up with pride. *At last, a new assignment! This one could get me to the top beside James Bond...although I still have to learn how to persuade beautiful women to force themselves on me. But now I'm going to a 'charm' school, get ready James to move aside.*

Moneylove could not draw back the wide smile on his full lips, closed, as they were stretched in a line across his narrow face. He stood still, at attention, with his flat chest thrust outward from his small-boned 161 cm tall body. *James Bond may be handsome, sexy, and have height and a perfect build, but I'm working to make my shoulders broader and my waist narrower. It won't be long before my physique is on par with James.*

"Are you with me Moneylove?"

"Yes sir."

The Chief smirked, and then frowned to hide it. "You are the only agent free of assignments at present. Smith is tied up and the others are catching up on paperwork for head office."

"Thank you Sir," Ernest mouthed.

His CEO ignored him and continued. "A suspected drug trafficker Gerard Robertson died recently in a car crash. For some time we've been trying to gather enough evidence to have him arrested. He was the owner of a large old-style house, a Queenslander, which has been turned into three residences. The whole top floor is now a large flat where Robertson lived, and the lower ground level has been divided into two smaller flats.

Inside the front door you are faced with stairs going up to the flat upstairs. Originally the only entrances into the two downstairs flats were through doors built into the walls on either side of the hallway, but a while back Robertson had outside doors build into both flats. He then closed up the hall door into flat two, but, for some personal reason left the door into flat one operational, so now flat two has its entrance on the outside of the building only, while flat one has two doors. You'll be in flat one.

Lucy Robertson, the daughter, who now occupies the upstairs flat, has found writing on the wall of her father's office, and other notes sticky-taped to the wall over his desk. Several were in some sort of code. One said 'Ice to be delivered. Payment received.'

Although she found other strange notations she did not understand, she claims it was only when she thought she heard someone moving around in her flat at night that she called the police. The police found no evidence of false entry but after a search, located drugs and money hidden inside a secret compartment at the back of one of the drawers of the filing cabinet. Now it's up to us to find the main players.

As I said, you'll be stationed in the empty downstairs flat one. The other ground level flat, is rented by two young men."

The Chief paused, narrowed his eyes and stared into Ernest's. "Your job is to keep alert. Quietly photograph anyone coming or going. I'm told a bench under a tree in the garden is fairly well concealed by low bushes so you could use that. Make notes of any cars parked nearby especially if they drive off hurriedly. Some may not yet know their supplier is dead. I have arranged for the staff to have your equipment ready...mobile phone, camera, recorder etc.

You'll have back-up that you can call on any time. Inform us immediately if anything unusual occurs. As I said, keep daily records of everything that's happening, including descriptions of all comers and goers, particularly to flat two. We know very little about the young men living there. A neighbour told the police they were often seen talking to Gerard Robertson. Once they heard a loud "argument between them, and what they believed were blows being exchanged". The Chief paused.

Take that glazed look off your face. Go home and pack, and don't forget anything I've said," loudly voiced the Chief.

"Never Sir...I never forget." *Neither would James. He always had everything he needed, even the most beautiful women, but my time will come. I'd be up there with him now, if it wasn't for that rotten crawler Smithy. He manages to take most of the credit for whatever I do. Thank goodness he's on another case.*

"And DON'T blow it!"

Moneylove stretched his body upwards. He believed it made him appear taller. "No Sir. You can rely on me."

The Chief gave a quick intake of breath before turning his face towards the papers on his desk as a mode of dismissal. Ernest left.

The following morning, the appointed police officer escort introduced Ernest to Lucy Robertson at her home.

Wow! She's beautiful.

Lucy stood very close to Ernest as she spoke. "You officers do such dangerous work. I really admire you. I rang the police when I found quite a bit of writing on the wall and other strange notes. There was a list of people's initials and amounts of money beside them, some with ticks and odd words that had no meaning for me. One section of the writing on the wall disturbed me though, and I reported it. It said, 'Ice bill paid. Make delivery.' I knew Dad had been investigated regarding drugs and I didn't want to be involved in any way, so ignored it all, but when I thought I heard someone creeping around in my flat I was frightened and called the police. Now you people have taken over, and I know the Drug Squad have a great reputation for getting results."

Ernest's concentration was going elsewhere. He was feeling heat rising to blotch his face as she looked with admiration into his eyes.

She added, "I have the keys to your flat. I'll show you around."

He sucked in his stomach muscles. *That exercise I've been doing down at the gym now puts me into James Bond class.* He followed her down the stairs, stumbling at times from too much concentration on Lucy's figure. No guilt crept into his brain though, only a feeling that he would not mention Lucy to his girlfriend, Estella, whenever Estella decided to come back to him from her mother's.

Once in the foyer at the base of the stairs, Lucy explained. "These stairs to my flat were originally an internal staircase to the upstairs bedrooms. When the renovations took place years ago, the original doors opening into the rooms downstairs through the foyer, were not necessary, so new front doors to both flats were built on the outside, facing the front garden. The main door is kept locked at night. I'm the only one now with a key to it."

Lucy continued. "When Flat 2 was rented out to strangers the original inside door was not only locked securely but had a plywood covering on the hall side which made the door invisible and secure, so no one in that rented flat could enter the foyer.

The old door into Flat 1 was untouched, as a relative once lived there and joined Dad upstairs for meals a lot of the time. There is a spy hole still in that door which is convenient now. You can look through it and see if anyone is in the hallway, and let me know."

Lucy's mobile phone rang. She gave it a glance as they entered the main entrance, before turning to again face Ernest. She smiled. Ernest held his breath as she briefly held her gaze. He blinked as she stepped closer to thrust his flat keys into his hand, before slowly walking away, checking her phone as she went. Ernest watched her mount the stairs and out of sight before he reluctantly entered his temporary accommodation.

Once inside his flat, Ernest, faithful to his training, checked every cupboard, under tables, chairs, and eventually beneath the bed. He also stood on a chair and checked the tops of the heavy light shades for any suspicious objects or recording devices. He found none.

The days passed slowly. He heard and saw nothing unusual. The highlight of his stay was when Lucy made brief visits, but she also had nothing to report. He kept a diary of each time he visited her, and noted early that it seemed impossible for any stranger to gain entrance to her upstairs flat, especially as, after the first scare, Lucy had changed the locks. He began to think she was probably having bad dreams, but was too kind to say so. Ernest would never upset a lady, especially as each night she invited him up for a drink, the type and amount he knew James Bond liked.

After five days of forwarding, by phone, his regular diary entries that said nothing of importance, his boss was getting impatient. *If nothing happens soon the Chief will recall me. That won't look good on my record, and that dirty rotten crawler Smithy will probably get some bonus, and have a go at me forever.*

Feeling depressed, he tried to comfort himself with the hope that his association with Lucy would continue. *Estella hasn't rung. I wonder what she's on her high horse about now. She's not too happy for some unknown reason, but that's Estella.* Searching amongst his belongings he drew out a James Bond film. He sat down comfortably to watch, enjoy, and pick up any hints he may have missed in his countless previous viewings. It was almost midnight when it finished. He clicked off the TV. In the silence that followed he heard a scraping sound followed by the murmur of a man's voice.

Careful to have turned off the overhead lights, he padded to the door to peer through the peephole. He almost gasped aloud when he saw Fonzo, one of the men from flat two, in the stairwell. He was creeping softly towards the stairs. Behind him Ernest could see a hole in the wall of the opposite flat from where he had obviously entered the hall. *Lucy said the original inside door was well sealed, but it looks as if they've found a way to open it. From here it looks as if the bottom half of the covering hiding the door on that wall has been cut out and put on hinges, to create an entrance into the hall, as the front door's locked.*

Fonzo held a small torch. With one hand half covering its light, he began silently creeping up the stairs.

Ernest, stumbling in the darkness, felt his way back to the table. He began frantically tapping it in an effort to quickly locate his phone, but could not. In his fumbling, while circling the table, his arm came into contact with the back of one of the chairs. It overturned, crashing to the floor with a loud bang. He hoped the man in the hall did not hear the noise. Ernest, with his heart now pounding, tried to think; then it came to him. He ran into the bedroom, turned on the light, and grabbed his phone from the side table. Nervous, and fearful for Lucy's safety, he quickly messaged headquarters for urgent assistance, as alone he could do nothing. With his heart pounding he sat down to wait. From habit he made notes in his folder on what he had seen.

Several knocks suddenly pounded on his front door. *'Bout time.* He flung open the door, but before he could slam it shut, Fonzo and his flatmate Grego were inside the room. A cold chill went through him. Their expressions were far from friendly.

"Looking through the peephole were you?" Fonzo loudly demanded. He savagely pushed Ernest, causing him to over-balance. He fell backwards, hitting the floor hard. His body shuddered with shock on the impact. He took several deep breaths. *I'm lucky. The carpet's thick.*

Grego drew a gun from his jacket pocket as Ernest tried to get up. He relaxed his body and lay still. Fonzo pulled out a cloth and some rope from a canvas bag he was holding. Knowing it would be useless to protest in any way, Ernest watched as his wrists were tied together in front of his body. His ankles were then tightly knotted together with more rope. As they began to force cloth into his mouth Ernest tried to squirm away, knowing it prevented him from shouting if the opportunity arose, but to no avail. Another strip of material was tied around his face to keep the gag in place, almost cutting off his air supply.

Grego disappeared into the bedroom and brought out one of Ernest's bed sheets.

What cheek! That sheet's my new one.

They covered him, and together carried him outside to their car; conveniently parked directly in front of Ernest's flat.

"You know the best spot to dump him, don't you Grego?"

Move Over

"Of course I do Fonzo...the river near where it runs into the sea. The high tide'll take him under real fast. It's real deep. I do all me fishin' there."

They swung Ernest up and crushed him into the open boot of their car. He kicked, but they forced his legs to bend and be pushed down sideways by the closing of the boot. He heard footsteps, then doors slamming. The motor spluttered into action and the car moved forward.

Now I know how James felt when he was tied up and squashed into some small space. But he lived to tell the tale and so will I. But I wish I wasn't hurting so much. My legs are all twisted and I think I'm lying on a tyre-lever or something. If I keep bouncing around in here it'll only get worse, and I don't want to look bad to Lucy. Although, a few bruises help a man in my job impress the women. Damn! I hate the smell of dead fish.

Ernest's head struck metal as the car braked to a sudden halt. He was stunned for a moment, but held his breath and the pain began to subside. He heard the car doors open and expected to see faces looking down at him almost immediately. He did not know how he could stop them throwing him in the river and tried to remember what James Bond did in the many tight corners he found himself in. The men did not seem to be in a hurry and Ernest could hear their raised voices. He strained to hear what they were saying.

"The tide's out, you dumb idiot! We'll have to come back later tonight when the full tide returns and is starting to turn. That's the best time, not now you stupid clot! It's strong and deep then and he'll be out in the ocean in seconds." Ernest heard doors slam and the car move again.

I must think of a way to get out of here. Ernest twisted his face side-on to scrape against the clasp on the strap holding the spare tyre in place. Slowly the strip of material holding the hand washer they had partly shoved into his mouth loosened. Rubbing it against his shoulder it fell to his chin. He spat out the remaining part of the cloth in disgust. Wriggling his body around and acquiring more bruises, Ernest then managed to bring his hands up to his face. With his teeth he loosened the rope and his hands were free.

Next time they stop I'll bang on the lid and yell to get attention from whoever's close by. If I could only get hold of that tyre-lever but I can't. I think it's now embedded in my back, and I can't twist around enough to untie my feet.

There was a screech of brakes as the car pulled up with a body-wrenching jerk. Ernest groaned, but the sound of shouting, of people running, plus a lot of mumbled words, were all welcome to his ears. One voice rose above the others.

"Oh no, I know that bossy voice. It's slime-ball Smithy, the crawler. What's he doing here?" Ernest muttered.

Ernest banged on the boot lid and shouted. It was flung open. Ernest sucked in the fresh air, but his heart sank as he found himself staring up into the face of John Smith, who was wearing a satisfied grin.

"Where have you been Ernie? I thought you were catching drug dealers not getting free rides in their car."

He turned to a constable behind him. "Come here Wallace and assist poor helpless Ernie to get out."

As his ankles were released and he was climbing out with the help of the police officer, Ernest glared at John Smith.

"How did you get here Smithy? I thought you were busy elsewhere."

"The chief knew something was not right when we didn't hear from you with those hourly phone calls that tell us nothing. Then we got that last one. You sounded upset old friend. I was free, so the chief asked me to come over and check things out. Lucky I did. We've got both druggies now. One's already admitted they went into Miss Robertson's flat because they had handed over a lot of money to her father, and were searching for drugs they'd paid for. We'll crack Robertson's code and arrest the big boys...no sweat. This'll be great on MY record."

The rotten swine! Now he'll make out to the Chief that if it had not been for him the case would never have been solved. If James had his honour stolen, he'd ride it out and in the end he would triumph over them all. That's what I'll be doing. In the meantime I'll go to more gym classes so I can floor any lawbreakers who try to tie me up again.

As the two men were being led away, Lucy walked up to them from where she had viewed the scene from her open doorway. John Smith, whose face was lit up by what he considered a charming, winning smile, moved forward quickly, to stand in front of Ernest. She ignored him and walked around him to face Ernest. She took his hand.

"Thank you so much Ernest." She fluttered her eyelashes. "You've been very brave. You're my hero. Please call in for a drink whenever you're in the area, which I hope will be soon." She suddenly flung her arms around him and kissed him. Surprise and pleasure mingled together, caused Ernest to give John Smith a two-finger salute behind Lucy's back.

"See you soon," she said as she left them.

Who cares about Smithy with his, 'I'm God's gift to women' belief? I've just had the beginnings of a James Bond thank you, and jealous Smithy didn't get a look in. Eat your heart out Smithy.

While a stunned John Smith stood motionless, Ernest decided to ask Lucy to make a separate report to the Chief. *This time Smithy won't be able to take ALL the credit for my work as he usually tries to do.*

Ernest wore his widest grin as he almost danced away. As he turned to leave he began to hum the James Bond theme song, that was a favourite of his; uncaring that no one, except himself, would recognise his rendition of it.

* * * * * * *

Mary Bella
made me believe
she was almost a saint,
'Till she stuck out her tongue
at the vicar in church

* * * * * * *

OUCH!
Spring is bursting out all over,
So are you, so shut up.

I HATE BEING LATE – FOR A NEW DATE

Watching the hall clock,
How I hate,
Watching the hall clock,
When I've got up late.

Dressin' to go out,
How I hate,
Dressin' to go out,
When I haven't ate.

Wobbling down the stairs,
How I hate,
Wobbling down the stairs,
When the heels are high.

Drivin' to the station,
How I hate,
Drivin' to the station,
'Cos walkin' makes me late.

Being told my train's late,
How I hate,
Being told my train's late,
When I've got this new date.

Watchin' other trains race by,
How I hate,
Watchin' other trains race by,
When mine they ain't.

Move Over

Boarding my train at last,
How I hate,
Boarding my train at last,
To find at each station, a stop it makes.

Stoppin' while on our way,
How I hate,
Stoppin' while on our way,
'Cos it makes me extra late.

Missing the first date,
How I hate,
Missing the first date,
'Cos I've turned up late.

Arriving gloomy at our set spot,
How I hate,
Arriving gloomy at our set spot,
But, he **did** wait! **Must be fate!**

MY OWN WORST ENEMY

'Never Norma, will I weaken yet again.'
'But Claire, I need your help,' cried Norma.
'No...to agree, I'd be insane,
To let you 'con' me ever again!'

'I thought you were my friend Claire,
'cos your help's so generously given.
So I don't want it all to end.
We've been such a successful pair.

'But, you keep pressuring me,
To keep having parties galore.
I'm out of my mind, that's for sure.
My father thinks I'm mad.

He says, 'Tupperware is not much good.
Look at the things your Mum brought.
She should've stayed with wood.
The lids of them don't crack or bend.'

'Listen Claire, I'll make it up to you,
At next-week's party at Lenny Lee's.
I promise you'll get new lids,
For the broken ones...for free.'

'No way...wild horses couldn't drag me there.
My cupboards are full to overflowing,
With uncountable intermixable items,
Plus 14 microwave dishes I never use.

There's also two picnic sets I never can find,
A cook book that I've mislaid, or lost,
Plus stackables galore.
All colour matched, of course.

Then there's the vegetable peelers,
All sizes and all shapes,
But I never seem to make them work,
The way I think they should.

So never ask me again to buy,
'Cos I have no room left to fill,
Not even a toothpick could I fit.
No parties, nor buying. It's over…no lie.

I now hear someone knocking Norma.
Why! your Avon lady has arrived,
With a bunch of goodies.
Let me take a look. WOW!

Perhaps on second thought,
I'll also have a set of those, in gold of course.
Bring it to Lee's party on Saturday.
See you there…'bye Norma, 'till then."

I'M MY OWN WORST ENEMY.

MOVE OVER! Assignment 3
Love not wanted

AT 6:45 am on this particular day, Ernest Moneylove found himself scrunched down between the two hibiscus bushes on the curb close to Bernice Wong's store. He stayed poised and mentally alert despite the irritation where the rough seams of his brand new khaki overalls, dragged and abraded along his inner thighs each time he tucked his legs closer to his body. *Should have washed them*, he conceded to himself. *Roughed them up a bit, dirtied them. It's hard to look like a tradesman squatting on the kerb waiting for a lift to work, wearing brand new clobber.*

He casually glanced around at Bernice's store, and his nose twitched at the sight of bulging rubbish bins, piles of discarded containers, and stacks of disused boxes scattered about the property at the side of the shop. *Ahh...a good place to hide drugs. As soon as Bernice makes a wrong move and leads me to them, it's on to rounding up the main player, and another step towards James Bond spy status, ahead of Smithy, the rotten crawler.*

He began to relive the conversation he had when he was summoned to the office of Mr Grant Stand, his Chief Executive Officer. "I know you're keen to move up the ranks in surveillance Moneylove, and the Drug Squad always values conscientiousness.' Ernest had beamed. 'Smithy's out on a secret mission so I'm giving you an undercover job...and don't blow it."

"No Sir...thank you Sir."

"To fill you in...several Asians who arrived in the country recently have been arrested on drug smuggling charges. Unfortunately this puts everyone on that same flight under suspicion. One of them, a Soonee Wong, who's on a temporary visa, is staying with his Aunt Bernice. She sells groceries, drinks, Chinese herbs and remedies. Your assignment is to keep a watch on them...but remember we're after the big guy."

The CEO fixed him with eyes narrowed. "Reckon you could handle it Ernest? It's the sort of thing careers can build on, so **don't** foul up.'

Moneylove recalled the delightful wrench in his gut as the CEO, for the first time, had called him by his first name. He wondered if Smithy, the 'favourite' was on such personal terms with the chief, but doubted it. *Smithy might get the best assignments, but I'll prove I'm the better agent.* He straightened his shoulders and lifted his chin higher.

"No Sir...Thank you Sir." Ernest's wide grin threatened to attack his ears as he tried to look Cool, Confident, and Capable; the three C's his CEO claimed were the hallmarks of his officers' successes. Ernest had no doubt that he was cool, confident and capable. He would land Mr Big Guy. It was 'in the bag' so to speak.

"What procedure do you have in mind Sir?"

"For you...a tradesman waiting outside Bernice Wong's shop for a lift to work, and then dropped off there again at night. You keep a low profile and note anything suspicious. Keep us informed of regular customers and anyone you have doubts about. Mick Carbello who's got the fish shop across the road, is your local contact if you need one. He says Bernice appears worried. Her nephew, who arrived recently in this country is rarely seen. He bunks down in a back room at the shop apparently, but Bernice lives elsewhere and arrives about 7am to open up, and...."

Ernest had stopped listening. His eyes glazed over as he planned his strategy - *6.45am set up position; 8.30, a second-hand Holden (not to arouse suspicion) drug squad car would pick me up. Then back again at 5.30 pm.*

Ernest's mental drift back was aborted by the encroaching clip clop of Bernice's sandals. He held the open book that he had cleverly thought to bring, and covered the lower part of his face with it. He watched her enter the store through the side door. A few moments later she re-appeared carrying a box of empty bottles. She deposited them on the ground beside the steps before going back inside.

Alert for her regular early morning visitor described to him by Carbello, Ernest had not long to wait. A lean, clean-cut, khaki-clad rider bumped his pushbike up over the gutter. He dismounted on entering Bernice's yard. He began to gather up the discarded bottles and place them in a basket on the handlebars of his bike. 'He usually hurried away,' Carbello had said. But not this time. He remained beside his bike, obviously waiting to see Bernice.

He doesn't fool me, dressed like a tradesman in new khaki overalls - an active participant in the drug scene no doubt.

Bernice re-appeared and handed him a white plastic bag. Ernest turned his head and leaned sideways in order to hear what was being said.

"Maurice, guard it well. It's getting more difficult to get the powder into Australia, and make sure Mr.Sing pays up. He's a bit forgetful. His other order hasn't arrived yet so if you don't meet the courier on the way, tell Mr Sing to expect it tomorrow."

"I'll pick up my supply then too."

She pressed money into his hand. "Call this a donation.'

Although the man mumbled something Ernest did not grasp, he jerked himself upright and almost jumped for joy. *At last...I've hit the jackpot. Can't wait to see Smithy's face when I get that promotion.* Rippling with the thrill of it all Ernest drew out his mobile phone. He quickly dialled through to the squad car driver, waiting in readiness. "Follow the man in khaki on the push-bike. He's just turned into North Street. He's delivering. Pick me up after you've nabbed him handing over the goods and collecting the money."

"Sure Ernest, we're on our way."

It was time for Ernest to move. Staying past his pick-up time would only raise suspicion. He forced himself to walk nonchalantly, with the intention of crossing the street to Carbello's, from where he would ring his boss in private. Suddenly his path was blocked by a middle-aged buxom woman with very short frizzy hair, who had somehow bounced around from behind to block his path. Her wide nose was flat - glued to a pockmarked face that looked as if it had been through a few bouts with the best American boxer. From beneath heavy drooping eyelids, the woman was staring at his clothes – his body? He felt alarmed that he had not noticed her coming, or heard her creep up on him. *Very un-James Bond of me.*

"The boss said you'd be wearing khaki," she lisped through protruding well-spaced teeth.

Trained to listen and encourage eager lips he agreed. "You're right. I am wearing khaki." *And so was the bike-rider. She must be the courier, and she thinks I'm the bloke on the bike.*

"I've got the order."

This is better than I dreamed. "Thanks, but I'm the new kid on the block so who do I thank?"

"Mr Ling Wei Fu, Importer. I think this stuff's some of his overseas junk."

"And you are?"

"Ethelynn," she shyly mouthed.

"You're his secretary?" *Flattery always helps.*

She giggled. "Nooo, I'm part of his domestic help. He sent me he says, 'cause I'm an adventurous spirit. He's right…I think…but I ain't had no adventures yet."

"I AM surprised," was Ernest's aside as he noticed the squad car entering the street. Ethelynn giggled with pleasure. "So what have you got for me?" he added.

Ethelynn plunged her plump hand into the depth of her large handbag and drew out a packet, which she handed to Ernest. His fingers prodded its contents from the outside. It was lumpy. *New method…but I'm up to their tricks. It's so you won't feel the powder.* He pocketed it as the office car came to a stop beside them.

The two men in the front nodded and winked at Ernest. He nodded back before facing Ethelynn. "We'll give you a lift back to your job Ethelynn, but I'll have to stop at the office first."

Giggling anew, Ethelynn managed to snort, "Ta."

Her large bulk began to press against him as she squeezed past him to enter the back seat of the car, causing her almost football-sized bosom to slap against him. He quivered. *How is it James gets all the beautiful, sexy young women, and I get this blot on womanhood?* Reluctantly he followed her. He seated himself as far as possible away from her, but she kept wriggling closer until one of her large hot legs scorched his. He was trapped.

He tried to direct his mind elsewhere. "Everything go well Siggie?" he enquired of the driver.

"Sure, we nabbed him in the act of handing over the packet and taking money off some old geezer. We got 'em both. Dropped 'em off at headquarters."

The other man cast his eyes in Ethelynn's direction. "Who's that?"

"Mr Big Guy's courier."

"The Big Fella couldn't have picked a better one. Never suspect her. Good work Ernest. The boss'll be pleased."

Ernest found it impossible to wallow in self-appreciation and self-praise. All his efforts were put into trying desperately to wriggle further away, to avoid suffocation from Ethelynn's hot garlic breath and warm throbbing body. It was to no avail. Sweat now glistened on his forehead. He tried to appear interested in the street outside but she insisted on talking. "Mr Ling's got lots of friends like youse."

"I don't think 'friends' is the right word," he muttered. He immediately lapsed into silence as he became aware Ethelynn was again running her questing eyes over his body. He shuddered. "Can't you drive faster?" suddenly demanded the now frantic Ernest.

"And get booked?"

"O.K, but do your best," Ernest grunted, as the car sped on.

Before the car had completely stopped in the office car park Ernest was out of the vehicle. He rushed into the main office and handed the packet to the C.E.O.'s secretary, requesting immediate attention by the C.E.O.

He was breathing heavily with excitement, anticipating a 'pat on the back' in the form of a promotion, and later a martini as James Bond liked it, *Move over James. I'm about to share the top spot with you.* When he was finally summoned into the boss's office, he bounced in. He could not control his excitement. "Good job I did, hey boss?" he announced.

The CEO's eyes narrowed, adding more gloom to his grim expression. Ernest's face drooped in response. He began to think that James would have the top spot longer.

"Good job?" Mr.Grant Stand raised his voice. "Good job! I should bill you for the time wasted...the embarrassment caused."

"But...but..." sputtered Ernest

The CEO leaned forward and spoke slowly as if to a small child. "Your drug courier turned out to be a

Maurice Goodfellow, a good-deed-a-day Boy Scout leader who picks up items, mostly bottles, for his group's fund-raising. He bike-rides to save the environment or something."

He picked up, waved an opened paper bag in front of Ernest's face, before turning it upside down. White powder spilt on to the desk. "This is what you had the troops pick up from Mr Sing. Do you know what this is?"

"Dope of some sort...heroin?" he hopefully managed to whisper.

"Rare powdered deer horn.... a supposed medicine for virility."

Ernest looked puzzled.

The Chief tossed the bag to one side, and sighed, muttering, "why me?" before continuing. ''Ask your mother. She'll explain it to you. Now pay attention. Once a month this Boy Scout fellow picks up deer horn powder Bernice Wong imports, along with ginseng for himself and Mr Sing. They both swear deer horn is the tops.

Moneylove felt embarrassed and hated it...not a James Bond thing. "But..." he sputtered, hopefully attempting to redeem himself. "The bike-rider could have gone into the shop for deer horn powder. Why the back door business?"

"Because it's quicker to have it ready for him when he arrives I suppose, and as for this."

The chief had swept up the open bag Ernest received from Ethelynn. He shook it upside down. Dried roots tumbled out. Ernest gasped. There was no powder with them, and the roots did not look like what the manual claimed the drug looked like. *Perhaps they've been hollowed out. Those drug barons are smart.*

His boss read his bewildered expression. "These are ginseng roots," He almost shouted. "They claim ginseng gives you extra strength. They also claim that taking both Ginseng and deer horn powder is the best combination since butter joined bread."

Ernest slid slowly into the chair opposite his chief. His expectations were vanishing; his dreams dissolving, but he struggled on. But...but...Bernice? What about those mysterious visits she's been making to the city?"

"She goes to the Department of Immigration to get an extension of her nephew's visa."

The CEO leaned closer to Ernest and became more intense. "Fortunately, we checked your ...err...investigation results, and thanks to Smithy, who has now replaced you, we found that what you managed to obtain in the way of evidence of a drug ring, were two items both legal in this country. If I had gone ahead with this I would have been laughed out of the Organisation."

Ernest cringed as his boss, now red in the face, shouted. "Moneylove, always make sure of your facts or call in your betters. Smith is always ready to assist you. Lift your game!" His voice dropped to a whisper. "Remember...we still have vacancies in Antarctica."

"Sorry sir. I'll do better next time." Ernest rose quickly to his feet. *Even James had his mishaps, but they were short lived, like mine will be.*

"Next time! Next time!" He sucked in his breath. "Oh yes, I do have a job for you. It's..."

"Oh thank you Sir for giving me another chance. I'll catch 'em this time." *I'll show that crawler Smithy.*

The C.E.O. gave a forced sideways grin of pleasure. "This job is to deliver that crazy, non-stop giggling Ethelynn back to wherever she came from. Her exuberance over her 'big adventure' as she calls it, is driving everyone in the office insane." Ernest's mouth gaped open in horror.

"Now get on with it!"

Ernest knocked his knee against the chair as he scrambled to escape. Limping through the door and into the passageway, Ernest's stomach turned in a sickening roll as he was confronted by Ethelynn's uninviting and grinning countenance. For a brief moment of fascination Ernest watched her tight black curls bounce like demented springs over her skull as she jerked her head up and down in greeting. He groaned and backed away as she walked towards him.

"I'm to drop you off home." He almost choked on the words.

"That'll be ni-ice." She gazed at him from heavy-hooded eyes as both hands reached out to encompass him. He recoiled, shocked as the realisation dawned. *Hell, she likes me.* The horror of being crushed in a bear hug by Ethelynn caused him to quickly brush past her, foiling any attempt by her to touch him. She followed behind him, so close he fancied he could feel her hot breath on the back of his neck. He increased his pace; fearful she might fall forward and crush him to death.

I wonder how I can get her to sit in the back seat while I drive. Tell her I've got something contagious?

Rabies? AIDS? Hell! James Bond never had problems like this.

Meanwhile, the Chief was grinning widely as he moved away from his half-opened door, from where he had been watching Ethelynn's bumbling attempts at gaining Ernest's interest.

"There's some satisfaction to be got in this job at times," he muttered.

On resuming his seat at his desk, he reached for the deer horn powder and dropped the packet into his brief case. As an after-thought, he also slipped in the ginseng.

The department won't miss it. I'll take it home. I'll be a young man again. Come to think of it, that bumbling Moneylove turns out useful at times.

* * * * * * * *

CONFUCIUS DIDN'T SAY:
He who get kicked in teeth,
must talk through clenched fists.

* * * * * * *

I even put his toothpaste on his brush
for him each morning,
Now he's left me.

LIFE'S JOURNEY

Around 2, many a mother has said,
'Never, Never, eat dirt,
Or spit out food. It's rude.'

Around 4, many a mother has said,
'Never, never, bite your brother,
No matter what he says.'

Around 6, many a preschool teacher has said,
'Never, never eat chalk,
Or kick the kids you hate.'

Around 8, many a strict father has said,
'Never, never, push away your food,
Beans and broccoli are good for you.'

Around 10, many a teacher has said,
Never, never, give me cheek,
Or you'll get a slap across the back.'

Around12, many a worried father has said,
'Never, never, disappear 'till after dark.
It makes our teatime late.'

Around 14, many a strict mother has said,
'Never, never go behind the shed,
With that boy from school again.'

Around 16, many a friend has said,
'Never look goose-eyed at him again,
He likes me, not you.'

Around 18, many a nun has said,
'Never, never, will you make,

Vera M. Murray

A pious nun…look to wed.'

Around 20, many a boyfriend has said,
'Never, never, will I marry you.'
So she cries a while, then finds another.

Around 24, many a boyfriend has said,
'Never, never, can I do without,
You and your wishy washy ways.'

Around 28, many a husband has said,
'Never, never will I lose the love,
For the wife and kids I've got.'

Around 40, many a woman has said,
'Never, never will I marry,
Any stupid man again.'

Around 50, many a new husband has said,
'Never ever will you be lonely when home alone,
I'll teach you rules for football, cricket.'

Around 60, many a bowls partner has said,
'Never, ever, will I play with you again,
You keep rolling bowls off the mat.'

Around 70, many a grown-up child has said,
'Never, never, will Mum cope alone,
The house is big, the stairs many.'

Around 75, many a grandchild has said.
'Never will grandma be the same,
She smiles sometimes, at our best advice.'

Around 80, many a great-grandkid has said,
'Never ever, will great-grandma
Seem anything but old, but she seems O.K.'

Around 80 plus, many an OLD ONE has said,
'Never ever do I want to leave 'never-never-land',
Where love is, and to me, my children stay children.

* * * * * * * *

The radiance of spring spreads like the perfume of lilies, through the house, through the garden, and through me.

A BATHROOM CRISIS

The cat has gone and done a bunk,
To save its nine, but what 'bout mine?
The blue tiled floor is all awash,
And saturated are my socks.

You see, I cannot get the plug,
From its outlet in my bath tub.
It's swollen, and will not budge,
While the cold tap's stuck on mega blast.

The water...it is rising fast.
I think it could become a flood.
I try to open up the door,
But it's stuck, so am I doomed?

This house, I just bought,
Is old, but got it cheap.
At the time, I gave a loud cheer.
Now I feel it was a rort.

For my neighbours, Will and wife.
I shout out, no, I screech,
Perhaps they're out somewhere,
And cannot hear my shrieks?

The clang of metal reaches me.
My fears subside. "I'm in here mate!"
My mistake! That was next door's gate.
I'm surely doomed...soon be too late.

If the worst comes to the worst
and I'm totally immersed,

And being too fat to float,
I'll drown. Wish I had a boat.

In bursts Will, come to rescue me.
How relieved can a woman be?
Gone is the fear of being cast,
Into the front yard while half clad.

I gave poor Will a mighty hug,
When a gurgling, sucking song was sung,
From the plug-hole he'd unplugged,
In my no more overflowing tub.

* * * * * * * *

A newborn baby only stays quiet,
'Till he spots a wide-eyed, open-mouthed relative.

* * * * * * * *

When carols ring out,
Coins clink, credit cards swish,
Mums sigh, children grin.

MOVE OVER! Assignment 4
A Drug Cocktail Made Ready

"SO nice to talk to someone not stoned out of their brain." I told Mr.Grant Stand, my CEO, who was only paying me a visit in person because he was short-staffed.

I, born Elfie Jones, now Ernest Moneylove, undercover member of the Drug Squad, but because I was working under-cover on this assignment, I'm called Mal Murphy. I was meeting my Chief, Mr Grant Stand, at a prearranged secluded spot within a quiet neighbourhood park. This was necessary, because I could not be seen fraternising with ordinary people, only with the derelict and drug-taking group I had infiltrated. It could blow my cover.

The Chief, having eyed my unshaven face, long hair, grubby clothes and dirty boots with distaste, was seated at one end of the park bench. I sat at the other. He also held a handkerchief to his face as the wind was not being sociable. We did not look at each other when we spoke, trying to appear as casual strangers.

"Let's not stay too long Moneylove, or rather Murphy. What have you got on the drug boss...the General?" He spoke crisply. "You should be close. You've been mixing with that low life long enough. Don't mess it up."

I ignored that, as my idol James Bond of movie fame would have, and replied. "Shouldn't be long. I've an appointment with the local supplier, Mr Wall. He's named Bull...short for bull terrier. He's called that because he never lets go of a client, unless they died or are broke. It's for tonight at 10pm at that boarding house I've moved into. His room's across from mine. As the plan is to find out who the General is it will be a cinch after I record on tape, Bull selling me drugs, plus whatever incriminating information, I can draw out of him."

"How did you get on to this...err...Bull?" The chief leaned forward with sudden interest.

"Through a half-dead junkie called 'Lucky'. He told me where the drug dealer lived, so I moved in there too. "

"Can you trust a junkie?"

"I just had to take the gamble."

The Chief was pleased. I could tell from his expression, even though he gruffly said, 'Bout' time too. You've been months on the streets and yet you haven't come up with any firm leads until now...hopefully you're right. At yesterday's briefing session it was suggested, that, as you seem to be getting nowhere, you should be replaced...new blood, new angle. John Smith's name came up, but unfortunately he's busy elsewhere. Nothing personal you understand."

The idea of giving up and going home to Estella who'd returned was temptation personified, but I resented the inference that I had failed my assignment. I made a guess that backstabbing Smithy was behind it somewhere. *Although I have nothing concrete as yet, I, like James Bond, never give up. Tonight's the break I've been waiting for.*

"I need a little more time," I said. After all, my plan was fool proof. I had a clear Bond grasp on it. "I'll be able to give you names after my visit to Bull tonight."

"Okay...but you'd better come up with the goods very soon, or, some other plan that WILL work."

"After tonight we'll be able to close in."

The Chief sighed as we silently parted, each in opposite directions. No need for 'good-byes'.

I pondered on what he said. For three months I had been on the streets, mixing with drug addicts and derelicts. I was living in a rundown guesthouse, unshaven most of the time, and with clothes needing a good wash or a trip to the rubbish bin. No one else would put their hand up for this assignment. I'd like to see Smithy take it on. He plays the waiting game.

It was 9.30 pm when I arrived back at the guesthouse. Not knowing whether or not I was being watched, I staggered a bit and mumbled away to myself as I made my way up the stairs and inside. There was no one in the passageway so I sidled up to Bull's room. I was 'casing the joint' as they say. I staggered sideways so I could lean over and press my ear to his closed door. Doors and walls in the old building were thin. If he were not alone, it meant he had suspicions about me and a reception committee could be waiting. If so it would be 'curtains' for me.

All was silence in his room, except for the clank of a bottle on a table, the clinking of several glasses, and the sound of them being filled. I smiled, but hoped these were not in advance of my visit. I always insist on mine being freshly poured and the glass turned round twice as

James likes it, but one has to suffer sometimes in this job. What it did show was that I was going to be treated as a guest, to soften me up, probably to discover where I got my 'present supply', and whether someone had moved into his territory. I had played my cards right so far.

I heard footsteps coming up the front stairs. I moved quickly away, and into my own room. I had to watch every move, in case I had unwittingly blown my cover. Through a narrow opening of my door I watched to see who was coming. It was Kandy, a well-known ageing prostitute and drug addict who worked the streets nearby. Her red, dyed, long hair, drawn back in a bun with fancy clips, was a pathetic attempt to look younger. She stared unblinking, from glazed eyes heavily outlined with makeup. Perspiration glistened on her forehead and she shivered as if cold. No gamble as to where she was heading.

She knocked three times, then twice, then three times, at intervals on Bull's door. This series was what uninvited people used and those who had no previous appointment, but, at the same time were known to Bull. *She must be desperate for a fix, to risk visiting Bull uninvited, unless the drinks are for her but I doubt that.* I knew from what Mad Molly, who rented the room adjoining Bull's, told me in bits and pieces, mostly through her eternal reciting of nursery rhymes, that anyone without enough cash for drugs was in for a rough time with Bull. Everyone around the streets knew Kandy was having trouble attracting customers.

I retreated from spying, to stretch out on the hard springless bed to await the sound of her footsteps in the passageway when she left Bull's room.

I unwittingly fell asleep. A singsong voice, loud over the sound of rushing water from the bathroom next door, woke me. It was Mad Molly at it again. She was singing a nursery rhyme in a high-pitched tone. This time it was 'Twinkle, Twinkle, Little Star. How I wonder what you are...' etc. She was emphasising the 'How I wonder what you are...' line over and over. Was she on to me? An agent has to read between the lines, and with Mad Molly I had begun to understand her double talk.

I recalled that when I first arrived she was sweeping the passageway and wiping doorknobs. She was wearing gloves and I discovered she wore them constantly, even when she went to the common bathroom. I remember going up to this tiny, frail woman and introducing myself

'Hello, I'm Mal Murphy...room 19. I'm new here." She had turned her wrinkled face up at me as she sucked in her lips between her toothless gums. In a squeaky voice she began reciting. 'Simple Simon met a pie man going to the fair. Simple Simon wants some pie. Are you Simple Simon?" She croaked, and I knew it was her laugh. As I got to know her I gleaned from lines she emphasised that she knew when Bull had visitors. I believed she had a clear idea of what went on in his room.

It was obvious she was not like the rest of us, so I smiled broadly and walked away. After that we were sort of friends. I was the only one she gave that lopsided grin to. I believed she was not as silly as she made out and could be a source of information, so after that I took her on several occasions for an ice cream at the corner shop and called her 'sister'.

Fully awake now, I pulled out my Rolex watch from the depth of my deep pants pocket. It was close to midnight. Cursing, I decided to go to Bull's room, although it was late. I figured that Kandy would have long gone. I hoped I had not blown it and would have to think up some excuse to give him for being late.

I could picture the Chief's face if I told him. 'I had this wonderful opportunity to bag the General and his cronies but I fell asleep.' I would never live it down and be off the team quick smart and Smithy would somersault with joy.

I hurried to Bull's door. To my surprise it was open. I looked around. When I saw no one in the passageway I entered the room. What I saw stopped me in my tracks and a shiver ran down my spine. I'd never seen dead people before. I think they were dead. Bull was stretched out on his back on the floor with a knife in his chest. An empty glass lay beside him.

Kandy was lying not far away from him. I felt sick and stared at the ceiling until my stomach settled down. My special training and devotion to Bond's films then took over. I stiffened and listened intently. Was someone still lurking in the room? The bathroom door was ajar and the room empty. There was nowhere anyone could hide.

'What a lucky break' I thought.

I went through Bull's pockets, taking receipts but ignored his wallet. I searched his desk drawers and found a diary and papers with names, numbers and supplies. Some were in code but that would not be hard for headquarters to break. I quietly slipped out of the building, unseen I thought, to a public phone and telephoned the Chief to give him my report.

"I thought you **might** do it." He sounded approving for once. "Looks like you've come up with the goods after all. I'll have our undercover courier pick them up. We have work to do." He sounded so excited you would have thought he had carried out this investigation all by himself. I was 'on a high' myself and wanted to leave immediately.

"I can't wait to be in my own bed tonight, between clean sheets," I told him."

"I know you must be impatient, but stay put. Leaving might make police suspicious and spoil everything." He quickly hung up before I could argue with him. Half an hour later the courier, who was Smithy, arrived. He was dressed like a bloke down on his luck, with old baggy clothes, worn hat and shoes but all spotless...a clean giveaway...but when he gave me the right password I handed over the papers I had hidden under the mattress.

While waiting to get the chief's okay, I was surprised by a knock on the door. When I opened it two police officers stood there. They looked me over, from my unshaven face down to my worn dirty boots, then back to my face. Their expressions were of contempt and disgust. Obviously they believed they were seeing another 'no-hoper'.

"Yeah?" I enquired, yawning.

"We're investigating the demise of a male and female in this building."

"Who?" I tried to look surprised, and shocked.

"Mr Wall and a female whom we believe was known as Kandy"

"Who? You mean the Bull?" They stared at me intently. "The Bull, that's what he's called around here. Didn't know he had a girlfriend though. He was no friend of mine."

They made no comment and went on "Perhaps you can help us in our investigation. Have you any idea why this Kandy woman would want to kill Mr Wall and then herself?"

"Naw...just seen 'em round sometimes. That's all."

"Did you see any strangers, or anyone living here, acting suspicious last night?"

I tried to look puzzled. "No," I said. "I can't help you."

"If you remember anything that might help let us know." He dropped his card on the table. He did not want to get too close to me.

"I sure will," I lied.

They looked me up and down again as they left. One muttered, 'Fat chance.'

I stretched out again on the unyielding mattress. I was bored and anxiously waiting for the call that said the squad had nabbed the General. If the raids had been carried out in the early hours of the morning I should be home by the afternoon.

I waited impatiently, growing more anxious as the time dragged on. I tried to concentrate on a picture of the chief giving me a promotion and perhaps a medal, until I dozed off from boredom.

I jumped back to awareness when a loud knock came on my door.

'I'm home and hosed,' I thought, but was dismayed to find the two police officers had returned. I stared blankly at them.

"You're Mal Murphy?"

"Yes, but I thought you knew that."

"We've been advised that you were seen near Mr Wall's door around midnight. There are stains on the floor, which lead back to this room. We would like to examine the shoes you were wearing last night."

My heart sank. In my haste I had been careful but obviously not careful enough. I had overlooked checking my shoes and also forgotten Molly, who knew everything that went on in the place.

"If Mad Molly told you anything I wouldn't take it seriously. She's not called Mad Molly for nothing."

"Perhaps...after saying she saw you go into Bull's room she did recite Humpty Dumpy had a great fall...but...your shoes."

The officers were watching me closely as I dragged them from under the bed. They put on gloves and gingerly turned them over. Both looked suspiciously at several stains on the soles -- something that I had failed to notice. I will make a note of that in my diary for future reference. *That is very un-Bond like.*

"This could be blood. We'd like you to come with us to the station while these are being examined."

I had no choice but to go with them.

Move Over

In the Station's interview room I was told to sit and wait, but after some time of being ignored I put my own question to the two detectives watching me. No doubt they were making certain I did not leave before they were ready to dismiss me.

"I didn't do anything so why am I here?"

"You probably know already." He gave a twist of his lips. "Mr Wall did not die from a stab wound. The knife blade was too short and slipped off his rib cage...plenty of blood but not deadly. And, he didn't die from the hit on the head sustained when he fell either. He died from poison."

"Poison!" I did not have to pretend surprise. It was genuine. I suddenly remembered the empty glass I had seen on the carpet beside Bull.

"Have you anything to add. Any information you would like to get off your chest as to what you were doing in the deceased's room at midnight."

"No sir," I replied.

A phone rang and one officer left and closed the door behind him. There was silence until he returned half an hour later. He wore a satisfied smirk. "Perhaps you would like to change your story about last night. Your shoes show blood, fresh blood on both. Will we find it once belonged to Mr Wall?"

Although he spoke light-heartedly, as if he was my friend and confidant, I was up to that trick. The stern expression in his eyes showed a man who got the answers he wanted, given time.

"I don't know anything officer."

"Well we're arresting you on suspicion of murder."

"But I had nothing to do with it." I protested loudly, as I realised I may not be home by dark. I needed help. *Stay cool like James does.*

"May I use the 'phone Sir?"

"One call only. If it's to a lawyer I doubt whether any lawyer would come within a mile of you until you're deloused."

I called Estella. She sounded pleased to hear my voice. I think so anyway.

"Don't be alarmed, but I have met with a minor set-back." The listening police officer smiled. "I've been arrested on suspicion of murder." There was no response from the other end, but I thought I heard suppressed laughter – probably from the TV. "Of course it's a mistake." I went on as I got a 'What have you done now?' "No, I haven't messed up. Will you get on to you-know-who to straighten it out so I can be home tonight?"

"Are you sure, very sure, everything will be all right?" She now sounded fed-up. Our relationship was getting shakey AGAIN, but as a fan of James Bond I could soon remedy that. I'm learning some of his moves.

"Of course, no sweat, I'll be home tonight...bye my love." Her receiver banged down.

The listening officer was grinning now. I wanted to punch him so hard he would not grin for a week.

I was confident that the Chief would have me out shortly, but I waited, and waited. I endured more questioning from the police who appeared convinced they had the goods on me. 'Robbery – for drugs or for drug money - gone wrong' would be the normal conclusion I expected they would make. The cards were stacked against me. *What's holding up the Chief?*

After a nightmarish almost sleepless twenty-four hours in a cold cell with several snoring drunks, Smith, now in a business suit, arrived to bail me out. Estella must have got the message to the Chief yesterday. W*hat took them so long?*

"You're free for the moment," was the Sergeant's parting words. "And don't leave your present address. Report back here next Monday for a hearing, that is, if we don't pick you up before then."

At the door I skipped down the few steps, landing on the footpath. I ran to catch up with the now mysteriously acting Smithy but he had disappeared. He must have been told not to wait around, but why? I was beginning to worry as I returned to the guesthouse. I wanted to ring the Chief to find out if they had arrested the General, but I may have been followed so I held myself back. All I could do was wait until the Chief let the police know I was an undercover drug squad member. Until then I would remain under suspicion, and be forced to return and stay at the guesthouse.

With plenty of time to think, I began to wonder if the Chief had forgotten me in the excitement. He showed he was not too concerned about any strain between Estella and me over this assignment. It had been a long stint for us both, straight after returning from her last visit to her mother's. Combined with the rising impatience at headquarters to get results, I put these doubts down to frustration and tried to dismiss them, but they stayed, hovering in the background of my brain.

I walked back and forth for what seemed the hundredth time when a knock came on the door. I jumped, then ran to the door, excited. 'At last!' I thought.

I swung the door open. My face dropped. It was mad Molly.

"You got arrested." Molly looked concerned.

"That's all right...no harm done." Then it dawned on me. "You were on walkabout too. Bull's door should not have been open. What did you see?"

"Tomato sauce."

"Tomato sauce? Oh, 'That's the colour of blood ...so you had a look?"

"Humpty dumpty sat on a wall, humpty dumpty had a great fall. All the king's horses and all the king's men couldn't put Humpty together again... "

So Bull must be humpty dumpty. I have to learn more. "Like an ice-cream?" I asked.

She took my arm with one of her gloved hands as we walked to the shop, where I bought the ice-creams. We returned to eat them while sitting on the front steps.

"What did you see Molly?"

"Humpty, dumpty sat on a wall..."

I interrupted her flow. "You saw Mr Wall. He's humpty dumpty isn't he, with his big round tummy, and he had a great fall? You saw the woman too, didn't you?"

"Asleep...she was sleeping beauty. He was making a noise. I think he was thirsty so I gave him a drink from a glass on the table." She took a deep breath. "Humpty

Dumpty had a great fall....no one can put him together again."

I realised that must have been where the poison came from...in that spare glass of wine. When Bull poured the drinks earlier, the one that he laced with slow poison must have been for me. I would have been back in my room before it took effect. I must have somehow blown my cover. Obviously he had been told of my meeting with the Chief. It would have to have been that drug addict, Lucky! He lives in parks most of the time. You can't trust anyone. Bull must have been ready if something I said, convinced him I was not genuine, or confirmed that what he had heard was genuine. I was horrified to think I could have been dead instead of that ill- fated two.

"You're a darling Molly." I rose to leave. As I stood up a swaying apparently drunken man bumped against me. He slipped a note into my back pocket.

I walked away from Molly and as she climbed the stairs into the building. I read the note. All it said was 'Ring Chief,' but that was enough to tell me that the operation had been successful -- no more secret meetings in parks. No more nights away from Estella.

I hurried to the street-corner telephone. I would have run but a running derelict would attract unwanted attention.

The Chief answered immediately, which surprised me. He probably thought it was the press wanting an interview.

Before he could say anything I spoke up, "I've got the whole picture now. I know what happened. Mad

Molly was the one who gave Bull the poison by accident, but don't bring her into it. Anyway, she always wears gloves." I then blurted out the whole story as I knew it. He listened, and to my annoyance said." I really didn't think YOU did it." He seemed to be smiling as he spoke.

"Thanks." I hoped I sounded pleased, not sarcastic.

He continued. "By the way, that prostitute died of a heart attack after an overdose from a mixture of drugs, which she found in the room. But now for the best news. The 'General' and his cronies have been arrested." His self-satisfaction was evident in his voice.

"Great. Have you got on to the police? I can't wait to leave here and get home."

"All arranged. The police have concluded it was both murder, and death by misadventure. Case against you has been dropped."

"At last...I'll come and see you tomorrow about a rise in my pay."

"Like hell you will." The Chief laughed and hung up.

One hour later I called Estella. I suggested we share a take-away dinner to celebrate. She seemed a bit put-out when I also asked her to pick it up before I got home. When I did arrive home she would not come near me until after an all-over clean up. We then seated ourselves together on the lounge, waiting for the evening news to come on. When it did, it was the 'news of the day' on all the television channels. I was excited and could hardly sit still, much to Estella's annoyance.

I leaned forward as the Chief, looking very self-satisfied, began to give a run-down on how his department had made this dangerous drug bust. I waited, breathless, to hear myself mentioned as he gave details of the arrest of the General and the disbanding of his organisation. To my disgust he added that it was the fine work of his men that made it possible. *MEN? ME! It was ME that did it all.* Then I nearly choked when I saw that crawler Smithy standing near the Chief. He was grinning madly as if he was the one who had done all the dirty work.

James Bond, that successful arch-spy and ladies' man never had to contend with such glory seekers undermining him. *If only I had his equipment...hmmm.*

Time for a drink, shaken, but not stirred. "You want one Estella?"

"NO thanks."

DAVE ON HIS MA-IN-LAW

They say that Ma-in-laws,
Rasp on you like a saw.
Mine's a bloody pain.
I don't think she's quite sane.

She gets on my goat,
The silly old soak,
Always on the plonk,
Until she's out...clonked.

Now, can you believe it?
Mumsie cried from in a fit,
'I'm feelin' kind of funny.
Me pills fell down the dunny.'

Mumsie's mean as dirt,
Loaded that's a cert,
But she won't spend it,
So I keep on forkin' out.

I'm going broke.
That's not a joke.
I've had enough.
It's got too tough.

But then I'm thinkin',
Life's short as blinkin'.
Me dear ma-in-law,
Ain't got much more.

Whenever she does croak,
I'll slurp her money,
Like golden honey,
'till there just ain't any.

RETIREMENT DREAM

Not today, not tomorrow.
Not this week,
But come July, I will retire.
The invisible rope that ties me,
To this present wearisome work,
Will be completely severed.

How wonderful it will be,
To be free on each and every day.
I'll watch the seasons change,
Not just get a glimpse,
Through lunch hour breaks,
And busy hurried weekends.

I'll have no need for clocks,
Nor train timetables,
Or strikes that make me late.
No more umbrellas forgotten,
Here, there and everywhere.
These and other worries gone.

Oh, to smell nature's scents,
From the garden...on the breeze.
When nature's mood changes,
And westerly winds begin to blow,
Or if the weather turns to rain,
I'll stay curled up inside.

In that leisurely position,
I'll decide the programme,
For that day and the next,
On what to do, or not to do,
And whether it should be hurried,
Or was too much of a flurry.

Vera M. Murray

After a good long rest,
I'll join an oldies club,
The one that suits me best,
I'll learn to play bingo and bowls.
And I'll give them info as well,
'Bout what I've learned upon the way.

"WHAT! Miss Dawson?
No I wasn't daydreaming,
On the boss' time.
Yes, I know the work's urgent.
Yes, I know what you're saying.
It's 'Get the show on the road...NOW!"

I sigh for July!

* * * * * * *

Double-line spacing means,
Each word rests in its own lake of space.

* * * * * * *

A bald spot is like a lie, the bigger it gets the harder it is to cover it up

MOVE OVER! Assignment 5
Death Beckons

"COME to my office...immediately, Moneylove," commanded Grant Stand, the Chief of the Drug Squad, through his intercom.

Ernest, delighted, hastened to the Chief's office. *Like James Bond I'm always in demand. The boss can't do without me. Thank goodness Smithy the crawler is not in the office. He'd be racing in before me, offering himself as the BEST...hah hah...drug squad agent ever.*

He was panting, from haste and excitement, when he entered the Chief's Office. His Chief, Grant Stand, now seated, was drumming his fingers on the desk.

"Where have you been? Away with the fairies as usual...day dreaming?"

Ernest remained silent, accustomed to his Chief's outbursts of impatience.

"I've got an assignment for you."

He relies on me. If it wasn't for that crawler Johnny Smith I'd have every assignment.

"Smith and the rest of the crew are involved in another investigation, so I have no choice but to give this assignment to you."

"Thank you sir." Moneylove stood at attention – his shoulders squared. *That gym work is really helping. I've gained two centimetres in height and three centimetres around my chest. They can't call me skinny any longer. Just because Smithy's build overshadows* mine, it doesn't come near James Bond's perfect physique.

"Are you listening?" grumbled the Chief, as he leaned back in his chair.

"Yes sir."

"What was supposed to be a reliable tip has resulted in the wrong man being arrested, or rather, he's only a minor player. You will see on the file he's on the pay roll, and a close associate, of Mr Pisaro. We know Pisaro is the main supplier/importer, but we've been unable to nail him so far. We heard whispers these two were partners. We expected this arrest would also result in roping in Mr Pisaro, but it's failed.

Although a large quantity of drugs was found in this man's possession, he claims he did not know they were there. He blamed some visitor. He's being held in custody though. Unfortunately we found nothing to connect him, by way of drugs, to his boss. John Smith isn't at fault. We all have the responsibility to act on tips."

Of course not! Your Golden Boy can't do anything wrong in your eyes. The damn crawler will meet his match someday. I look forward to that.

"To save the good reputation of this division of the Drug Squad we have to arrest the main importer/supplier. He is known in the trade as Lordie Lordie. They use this nickname in their conversations so no one will catch on to whom they're talking about. We believe Pisaro is Lordie Lordie.

We discovered Pisaro spends his weekends on Straitbreak Island. As you're the only one available, I have to send you to the island on this assignment. SO

DON'T BLOW IT!"

"I won't sir," Moneylove loudly uttered, puffing out his flat chest as his small frame was stretched a further several millimetres towards the ceiling.

"You must report daily to this office. Record any suspicious activities and any gatherings that look more like a meeting than a social get-together. The manager, who wants to keep his hotel's good reputation, will be of great help. You will be in the guise of an employee. Of course, you'll have a room as you may be called on any time, day or night."

Stay at the Pinnacle on famous Straitbreak Island! At last my value is being recognised. At last I'm getting the same treatment as James Bond.... staying in a first class hotel. Of course, this comes with beautiful girls. Smithy'll be livid when he finds out. Ernest allowed himself to give a tight-lipped grin at the thought.

"Don't get carried away. You have a lot of work ahead of you. You'll have to be alert at all times. You'll work in with the manager. He wants the matter cleared up quickly before rumours spread. There is always such talk eventually, and it could ruin his tourist trade.

Go and get your things, and remember to keep us informed at all times."

"YES SIR!" Moneylove stepped back quickly and tripped as his foot kicked the leg of the table. The Chief sighed and lowered his face to concentrate on the papers on his desk.

Ernest, limping, collected what he needed from the office – his trusted radio, mobile phone, pen torch, and some James Bond DVDs. *There'll be a player in every room of such a posh hotel.*

That afternoon Ernest arrived, via barge and bus, at the hotel. The manager Mr Roland Stubbs was waiting in the foyer. Ernest walked in slowly, still feeling the effects of the seasickness he suffered on the barge coming across from the mainland. Mr Stubbs came forward, grabbed his hand and shook it vigorously. Moneylove flinched and was relieved when he managed to withdraw it. He resisted the urge to rub it.

"I'm so pleased to have you here, Mr Moneylove. Come to my office.   Leave your bags on the floor here. You can get them later."

Mr Stubbs walked so quickly Moneylove failed to keep up with him, lagging several steps behind. When he was partially inside the office, its automatic door, as it closed swiftly, caught the edge of his left heel. He jerked it awkwardly away.

"Did your superior tell you everything? You are to pose as an employee, on duty at any time, as directed by me. Officially you will be on the books as a waiter/room-service attendant. Wally our head-waiter is waiting to take you to your room in the employees' section behind the kitchen."

What! A room behind the kitchen...not one with a view of the ocean and room service at the press of a button. I've been cheated. Ernest sighed deeply. *But James Bond has his setbacks and ends up a winner, comforted of course by his beautiful assistants. I'll never let that smart-alec Smithy know I was on the same level as a servant here. He'd never let me forget it. Like James, I'll use this setting and remain incognito in order to outsmart that drug importer. I'll show that Smithy.*

"As for the suspect you are investigating, Mr Pisaro, most of his weekends are spent here at this hotel. He and the friends who accompany him, enjoy sailing and swimming from the beachfront near the jetty. When not at sea, his yacht is anchored beside the pontoon situated in front of and on a level lower than the hotel grounds.'

He walked towards Moneylove and slapped him on the back. 'Time now for you to get unpacked and settle in."

Ernest exited the office ensuring that his heel did not get trapped in the door.

On the Saturday following his arrival, Moneylove watched as Mr Pisaro arrived with a beautiful female companion, and other guests. These included a business associate, Sandy Walldrop, who was accompanied by a tall blonde who possessed a figure that mesmerised Ernest. He could not look away. He was pleased his Estella was not present. She would not have spoken to him for days.

When Mr Pisaro was away from the hotel area, it was with his forever smiling, willowy girlfriend and his other friends, on his yacht. On the evening of their return from their ocean jaunt, he would give a special dinner for his guests.

On that night Ernest was placed on duty helping to serve at Pisaro's table. Watching closely, Ernest decided to record for the Chief that Pisaro and his male friends, with their olive skin and dark hair and eyes, appeared to be members of the same family. Moneylove recalled the picture of the man arrested. He had a similar appearance.

Like James Bond, as he stood beside the table, Ernest glanced out of the corner of his eye at each guest. There were four men and four model-shaped and expensively outfitted young women. One activity surprised Ernest. He noticed that Mr Walldrop and Mr Pisaro had girlfriends who had different tastes in clothes but carried large black, almost identical handbags. On the front of one was a large gold clip, while the other bag had a large silver clip.

Estella would never carry a large handbag like that when dressed up. Perhaps they have their beauty kits inside to repair their makeup when they go, always together, to the ladies toilet.

The second Saturday night arrived and Moneylove was exasperated. His boss had been continually contacting him, almost demanding he quickly finalise the investigation. The Chief wanted quick results as a court case was looming, brought on by Pete Pisaro's lawyers on behalf of his arrested employee.

Thank goodness I was not involved in that case. Sneaky Smithy would have blamed me in some way.

The dinner went without incident. Ernest noticed the same manoeuvring by the two girls who seemed to have exchanged handbags after a visit to the 'ladies'. Something disturbed Ernest but he could not put his finger on it.

As he was collecting empty glasses, several of the guests were whispering together. He caught one word, "Lordie". *Jackpot!* He hurried back to the kitchen and spoke to the superintendent. 'I'm going to my room.' He was dismissed with a nod.

Ernest now knew that, to get any evidence against Pisaro, he would have to look further. He quickly sent his Chief a message informing him that he was now leaving his room to search the yacht.

He changed into black clothes. True to his training he collected his torch, mobile phone and recorder and put them in his pockets.

As he hurried down the walkway to the yacht, he wondered if any employees were on guard. When he stood close to the yacht he heard and saw no one. He climbed on board noiselessly, should, by chance, there be someone below deck.

Padding quietly on his thick-soled sneakers, he scanned inside the sleeping quarters, then the dining area, but he found nothing of interest. He cursed that he had not brought something to force open the many drawers that were securely locked. He returned to the wheel area and again found nothing.

Back on deck he began to look for any containers beneath the benches attached to the rails. He stooped to pull away a large folded tarpaulin pushed carelessly beneath one of the long benches. Voices drifted down to him from the walkway. He froze as the sound of their footsteps drew louder. He realised two men were heading towards the yacht.

He looked around for some place to hide. His heart pumped loudly. *Don't panic. Stay calm as James always does, no matter how desperate the situation.* Jumping overboard occurred to him, but he dismissed the idea. *Sorry James but I've never learned to swim...not yet.*

The voices drew closer. Desperation began to take over. *Where can I hide?* The bench before him seemed to be the only answer. He jerked out the large folded tarp. It gave him enough room to hastily crawl under the seat. Once there, he stretched out and pulled the tarp back to block any view of him from those arriving. He turned on his pen torch, pulled his mobile from his pocket; set it to silent, then texted a message to head office. He switched on his recorder. He lay still, breathing slowly and silently.

The sound of footsteps was now closer and the voices had become clearer. Ernest held his recorder close to a small gap in the overhead rungs of the seat.

"Lordie Lordie is having a good time, but I hope he doesn't stay away too long. Sometimes he does, to make sure the mules change the money purse for the drug purse. I want to get back to the mainland and me wife. We've finished what we came to do. That was a corker wasn't it? The buoy covering the crab pot containing the drugs was right where it was supposed to be. Once we pulled up the wrong one. The crabs were beaut though. You weren't here then. Some Asian bloke worked this scheme out with Pisaro. I must say it's brilliant...too damn clever for the drug cops to find out. They...."

The voices faded. Ernest turned off his recorder. Except for the gentle murmer of the ocean, silence reigned. Ernest, now resting comfortably, was unable to stop drifting off to sleep.

A loud voice broke into Ernest's sleep.

"I'm sure I heard snoring," it said.

Ernest was awake immediately, and for a few seconds wondered where he was. He soon realised the danger he was in. *I'll fight them barehanded if I have to.*

The tarp was jerked away despite Ernest clinging to it with all his strength. Strong rough hands grabbed a leg and arm and began pulling him out.

"Here's one for the sharks," said one of the men as Ernest's head became visible to them.

"Toss him over the side before Lordie Lordie returns. He'll kill us if he finds out we left the yacht together."

"Yeah! You're right. This way no-one'll know."

They pulled the struggling Ernest well away from the bench. As he squirmed they had difficulty lifting him to his feet, but he was no match for the two stronger men. They forced him to stand upright, while one held his arms behind his back. Ernest struggled desperately as they pushed him towards the rail. It was to no avail.

"Give him a crack over the head and knock him out before we heave him over," one suggested.

"Good idea."

I hope the phone and recorder are waterproof. They'll find them on my body when I'm washed up on the beach tomorrow...a hero.

Suddenly a strong searchlight lit up Ernest and the men holding him. A voice through a loud speaker announced. "You're under arrest. We have you covered. Let the man go. Don't be stupid and be up for murder."

That seemed to register with the two men. They

released Ernest who ran and jumped from the yacht to the pontoon. He then scrambled as fast as he could up the ramp. At the top he stopped. Behind the glare of the light, he came face to face with John Smith. He was standing, legs apart, on the top step of the walkway. He wore a satisfied grin on his face.

"Aren't you glad I came to rescue you...no? You can't help it, I know, but you never seem delighted that I'm always ready to help."

"Help!" Ernest was calm but furious. "All you do is try to undercut me."

"That's not true. You're too imaginative. I'm just a better drug squad agent than you. I'm just doing my job, like I was on that first investigation. That result wasn't my fault, but everything's sweet now with the boss. He'll probably give me a raise for what I've done here. You should be grateful. After all, I rescued you from being drowned or shot." Smith's manner showed a great deal of pleasure as he talked down to his shorter colleague.

Ernest managed to keep his anger in check...his lips sealed. His nerves began to settle down as he slowly realised that he had evidence that Smithy did not. He began to wonder just how much work Smith had really carried out.

"Well Smithy, what about Pisaro? Has he been arrested?"

"Not yet...I just had to come to rescue you first, my dear...dear...friend.' He was smirking. 'We have yet to get evidence that it was his drugs..."

Smith's mobile phone rang. He put it to his ear, listened, and then smiled. The call was short. He returned the phone to his pocket as he turned to face Ernest.

"Our men have found drugs on the yacht. But to continue...we cannot arrest Pisaro if he claims he knows nothing about drugs on his vessel. He's certain to say that they must have been hidden there, unknown to him... probably blame the crew."

For a few seconds Ernest's heart sank, but then he recalled what he had recorded. He smiled. *It'll be me who'll bring in the evidence that will be Pisaro's downfall. This time Smithy's crawling will not be much help. Although the boss will still give him credit that he doesn't deserve, perhaps the boss will give ME a raise.*

Ernest began to move away. *I'll go to the bar and celebrate my success with a martini, shaken not stirred.*

"What's that stupid grin for," snarled Smith.

"That's for me to know and you to find out." Ernest strutted away with his head in the air.

Move over James Bond, I've almost reached the top with you.

THE BATTLE OF THE BULGE

The battle of the bulge
Is what it's called.
And it sure is a battle.
I would say a curse.

Once trim and terrific,
Then fat and forty.
Now in life's later stage,
I'm well…err…chubby.

It's not that I haven't tried,
My weight to bring down.
I began with the grapefruit diet,
But didn't like the taste.

Then I munched on every brand,
Of wholemeal bread and buns,
That had no sugar, carbs, or salt,
'Till l felt, I was half starved.

I tried Weight Watchers for a miracle,
But I found no joy there either.
Maybe 'cos I could never recall,
Where I put their last article?

Then my daughter said to me,
"You've put the weight back on.
You'll soon be waddling like a duck.
Try Jennie Craig." And so I did.

I ate their rolls and lost my stack.
It melted from my ribs and bum.
Then I stopped. The deed was done!
But pretty soon the bulge was back.

Move Over

My Doctor gave me tabs to take,
To curb my appetite.
They kept me up all through the night,
So pitched them out of sight.

Then on to indoor exercise,
Until I strained my back.
That forced me then to cease.
I won't go back to that.

Then walking was the rage.
I puffed and blew a gale,
As I raced up hill and down dale,
Chased by some loose or lost dog.

When winter came at last,
With mornings dark,
And evening's cold,
My bed both warm and cosy.

But I haven't given up you see.
There's 'Light and Easy' on my list,
While Terry White the chemist,
Has a magic drink that may assist.

I see new diets by the score,
Like the LA weight loss group,
Are sold in many a store,
With promises galore.
Habits are hard to break,
Is what I've heard before,
But **now, at last,** I know for sure,
I have **NO** problem with my size.

I found the answer that I seek,

Vera M. Murray

> In shopping centres close by me,
> Where I can buy you see,
> From stores whose clothes don't cheat.
>
> Millar's apparel now is my choice,
> 'Cos I fit their size fourteen.
> Those other stores are incorrect,
> When they tell me I'm a twenty.
>
> NOW, when I walk I bounce a bit,
> But that just shows I'm fit.
> I'm so happy now, with no concerns,
> When buying food from KFC.

* * * * * * *

If we don't succeed in getting rid of those love-handles,
we run the risk of failure as a model.
Did I say that?

SENIOR LADIES HEALTH WALK

Oh dear! oh dear!
It's barely dawn.
The sun's not up,
And I'm forlorn.

I hear a knock.
My friend has come,
To walk ten blocks.
Where are my socks?

We're past our prime,
Know in our minds,
These walks a must,
To halt the rust.

In pre-dawn light,
We make a sight,
Thick pants, track tops,
Scarfs, gloves, long socks.

The air is crisp.
The breeze assists.
Our noses freeze.
We start to wheeze!

At first we jog,
So full of zest,
But gasp for breath,
On each hill's crest.

We slow our pace.
We puff past stores,

Vera M. Murray

As owners yawn,
At opening doors.

In dawn's soft light,
From a new sun,
We push with might,
Now home's in sight.

We say 'Hur-ray'.
She walks away.
I start to think,
Of forty winks.

The joggers off,
The corns relieved.
I brush my locks.
I toss my socks.

From my bedroom,
I hear her roar.
'Morrow mornin',
We'll do more walkin'...'

I cannot hear the rest she says,
I'm 'neath the blankets on my bed,
But I mutter, "I'll be ready,
I'm not decrepit yet...NOT ME!

MOVE OVER! Assignment 6
A Wrong and Dangerous Path

"WHERE is that dummy? Why doesn't he answer my summons?" shouted the Chief Executive Officer of the Drug Squad Division, Mr Grant Stand, through his partly opened office door.

The staff in the main office bowed their heads over their computers and said nothing.

Mr Stand shouted again. This time he was facing the closest clerk, Neil Webber. "Where IS Moneylove?"

Neil, forced to reply, said. "He's at morning tea Sir. He's not back yet."

The outside office door suddenly swung open. Ernest entered, holding a lamington cake in one hand. His eyes bulged as he saw his Chief's angry glare directed at him.

He would want me...the first time for ages. Just because that sneaky crawler Smithy isn't in, he probably wants me to wipe down his desk or something.

"Into my office immediately Moneylove."

"Yes Sir."

The Chief retreated behind his closing door.

"You're in for it now, Moneylove." A workmate stated the obvious.

Moneylove was about to march towards his Chief's office door when he realized he was still holding his uneaten lamington cake.

"MONEYLOVE!"

Ernest's body gave a light jump. He looked at the lamington. There was no time to take it to his desk and put it away. As he walked forward he stuffed the cake between his wide lips and tried to quickly chew and swallow it. He had mostly succeeded when he pushed open the Chief's office door and entered.

"Yes Sir," he mumbled through his cake-filled mouth.

Mr Stand stared at Ernest. "What are those black smudges and white flecks on your face Moneylove?"

"A lamington, chocolate icing and coconut coating," mumbled the embarrassed Ernest as he dug his sticky hand into his pocket. He withdrew a large handkerchief and began to vigorously scrub his face.

Mr Grant Stand sighed and muttered something too low to be heard by Ernest, before raising his voice once again. "As you are the only one available, and the Commander-in-Chief wants immediate action, I have no alternative but to send you on this mission. As you know, John Smith is unfortunately unavailable at the moment."

That damn Smithy again. I hope he gets lost somewhere, forever. "Thank you, thank you Sir," responded Ernest quickly, while straightening his shoulders and stretching himself upward to appear taller. *This may be the assignment that puts me up there on the pinnacle with James. That'll take know-all "kiss the boss's feet" Smithy, way down in the department's eyes.* "YES SIR," repeated the now physically relaxed Ernest.

"Keep quiet and pay attention to what I'm saying. There's a Carl Mingos. He travels a lot they tell us...stopping at various countries and spending short stays here and there, and always seen in company of suspect people. He's a representative, and part-owner, of an importing company. The British also believe him to be the leader of a drug cartel. The trouble is no one has yet been able to catch him. No drugs or drug dealings, although suspected, can be pinned on him.

We have received notice from Customs that his code name and number, which they obtained from somewhere, were in a parcel arriving here recently. In the package, drugs were found inside a toy teddy bear. This is not sufficient to prove he's even involved, as he could deny any knowledge of the parcel, as it was not addressed to him. Australia appears to be a planned extension of his operations, but we need more proof…proof that our overseas counterparts haven't been able to obtain.

He's bought a house here, and we have reports from a neighbour across the road, a Mrs Webcott, that, since he moved in, traffic has increased to an annoying level. She says that some of the guests at his weekend gatherings leave in a state that gives the impression of being under the influence of more than alcohol. She believes drugs are involved.

One house next door to Carl Mingos belongs to Liddy and Doug Lynch, a quiet couple. On the other side lives a recently divorced lady…glamorous and rich. She is showing a great deal of interest in Mr Mingos and attends the gatherings he has regularly."

This time I'll do the James Bond thing. I'll get the villain and use 'James Bond charm' to get the beautiful girl. There has to be at least one at these parties. A slight smile of excitement passed over his lips. *This will be a sweet and sour case…sweet for me, and sour for Smithy.*

"Pay attention Moneylove. I'm not going to repeat all this a second time. To trick Mingos we have created a new occupant on the ground floor of the building from which he conducts his business. It's called *Isis Importers*

Exporters. Signs have gone up and we have put one of our office girls in charge to receive any calls, although none are likely. This will be the background for your new identity."

I'll be a manager...that's one in the eye for Smithy.

The Chief noticed Ernest's cocky tilt of the head and muttered. "It's a pity that Smith isn't back."

Yes, what a pity that Smithy isn't here to lick your boots. When I'm sharing the pinnacle of success with James Bond, you'll have to put me first.

"Moneylove, don't go to sleep on me. As this man is under suspicion of being a drug supplier of giant proportions, you will keep us regularly informed of all that's going on, and photograph any suspicious visitors. Mrs. Webcott thinks she may be able to get you into one of Mingos' gatherings. She knows you will be under of the guise of being part of an importing company, with interest also in a shipping line.

You will be given all the necessary instructions and information on the fake Isis Company, as you pose as their filing clerk-cum-office boy."

Damn...I bet Smith would have been put up as the manager.

"Go home, pack your things and move into Mrs Webcott's house after seven tonight...less fanfare the better. Have you got that Moneylove?"

"Yes SIR," spoke up Ernest but he refrained from standing at attention and clicking his heels together.

"And DON'T BLOW IT...Go!"

Ernest backed into the outer office. There he received all the necessary information on the planned operation. He also collected what else he needed:

camera, recorder, and petty cash. With a steely gaze directed straight ahead, and with longer than usual strides, he left.

At exactly seven that Friday night, Ernest thumped his heavy suitcase up the sixteen steps at the front of Mrs Webcott's house.

The front door opened before he could reach the bell. A tall, well-endowed past-middle-aged lady faced him. 'You must be Ernest. What a good surname…Moneylove. Do come in. I'm Mrs Webcott, but you must call me Lorna.'

Before Ernest could reply, she had taken his arm and almost dragged him inside. Still clutching his heavy suitcase, he stumbled. He would have fallen on Mrs Webcot had she not being quick enough to jerk him upright and shove him backwards into one of the lounge chairs.

As he tried to settle into a comfortable position, Mrs Webcott said, "You must be tired, Ernest, working all day catching crooks. You relax there and I'll make you a cup of tea, and we'll have a yarn. Then I'll show you to your room. It's the one facing directly at Mingos' house. You'll get a good view from there." She tapped his knee and said, 'You'll see I'm right about weird and noisy behaviour."

"Well, I would like…" began Ernest, but Mrs Webcott had disappeared into the kitchen.

After several cups of tea, small cakes, and Lorna's minute-by-minute description of anything and everything connected to Mr Mingos, Ernest found it hard to stay awake.

It struck midnight when Ernest had finished unpacking, setting up his camera at the window, placing the recorder close by, and the mobile phone beside his bed. He was pleased there was no sign of activity at the house across the street. He was so tired he did not even think of Estella as he covered himself with the eiderdown.

The following morning, Lorna, who informed Ernest that her husband was away on a surveying job, told him she liked cooking and set out a large meal before him. He secretly wished Estella was the same, as he grew tired of making his own breakfast each morning.

As the weekend began to unfold, it was apparent that Mr Mingos was busy. They saw him leave several times for short absences. Two men arrived at the house before lunch. Ernest took a photo of all who came and went. The camera range also covered the two houses on either side of Carl Mingos' residence.

The following day, while standing with Ernest looking through the lace curtained window, Lorna pointed to a car outside the house on the right of Carl Mingos'. "That's Liddy going shopping. She and her husband Doug are a quiet couple and keep very much to themselves. She told me once she's fed up with Carl's noisy Saturday gatherings...mainly the noise of cars arriving and leaving. Doug is not well, but he does go out sometimes, usually with Liddy. You can't miss him though when he does go out. He's plump and has a mop of unruly hair and a mouthful of teeth.

By the way I've invited Mingos' other neighbour over to meet you", Lorna continued. "She's that rich girl, Anita. I've already told her you're a businessman in an importing company. Why...there's Anita coming across now."

Move Over

Ernest almost gasped at the tall blonde beauty as she entered the house. That she was taller than he did not worry him. Lorna directed them to sit together on the double lounge chair. Ernest half grinned in delight. *James Bond, I'm getting the beautiful girl now. You can't have them all.*

As Anita did not seem impressed by Ernest when she was introduced, Lorna realized that all was not going well. She decided to move things along. "Ernest, tell Anita about what you do. I know she'll be interested."

"Oh yes," said Ernest, dragging his eyes away from Anita's full bright red lips. *I'm sure I can get to the next level with this one.*

Ernest began to expand on his false position in his fake brother-in-law's importing/exporting firm. He added that he had complete access to all private data.

"Carl, my next door neighbour, may like to meet you. You two would have a lot in common, I think. I'll tell Carl and I know it'll be okay to invite you over to meet him, so I'm doing that now. Be at Carl's tomorrow night at around eight. I'll let him know you're coming."

Get ready James Bond. I'm on the first step up.

At 8 pm exactly, Ernest arrived at Carl Mingos' house, where Carl was at the door greeting his guests. He shook Ernest's hand vigorously when he arrived.

"So pleased to meet you. Anita tells me you're in the same business as myself. Perhaps we may be able to do business together. I need more avenues here to get goods on the move, so to speak. But go in and get yourself a drink." Ernest moved away as another guest arrived.

Ernest found the lounge room to be large and included a bar. He looked for Anita but could not see her anywhere. He wanted to investigate as much as he could, especially where the exits where, should a speedy disappearance become necessary. Having satisfied himself he had memorised all the visual details, he walked up to one guest. "Where do I find the washroom? I've already had too much to drink."

The man pointed to a door in the centre of the wall on their right. "Go through there, and it's at the end of the hallway."

Ernest glanced around. No one was looking in his direction so he quickly walked through the door the man had indicated. He entered a long passageway. A door on his left was locked, but further down was a door on the opposite wall. No one was in sight so Ernest opened it slowly and peered through. He found himself looking directly into Carl's garage. *Handy escape route if needs be.*

Ernest returned to the lounge. For appearance sake, he started mingling with other guests. They were now in small groups, talking and picking at nibblers spread out on small tables set up close to the bar.

Ernest noticed two men walking towards the passageway door. *Men don't usually go to the toilet together...not like women.* Ernest decided to follow, but wondered how he could without being noticed. *What would James do?* Before he could further puzzle over that question, a tall blonde stopped the two men. They moved closer to her and a conversation ensued. Their backs were now facing the door.

He quickly passed the trio and exited the room. Walking swiftly down the hall, he entered the toilet. He decided he might be discovered if he hid in a closed cubicle. Looking around he spied a tall storage cabinet. Opening it, he found one side held a set of shelves, the

Move Over

other hanging space. Without another thought he squeezed into the empty coat-hanging side. Cramped and sweating from a limited airflow, Ernest hoped the men would not be long. The sound of a door opening, then voices, made him sigh with relief. He listened intently. He heard one say, "This place's empty, but I won't give you the goods here. Carl would be ropeable if he found out. I'll meet you outside on the street in about a quarter of an hour."

"Okay," was the reply.

"Got ya," muttered Ernest. When he heard the men leave, he pushed the cupboard door open. After several deep breaths he telephoned the office with the news. He knew that whoever was on standby would pass it on to the police.

Ernest returned to the lounge. Delighted with his achievement he started a conversation with one of the female guests, as he could still not see Anita.

The screeching of car tyres caused everyone to halt what they were doing to hurry outside to stand along the balcony to investigate. Ernest joined them. Several police cars had zoomed in on two men standing between two parked cars. He watched the men being searched. He heard one say, before he was taken away, that he had brought the drugs to try and sell at the party. A quick but thorough search of the house, at Carl's invitation, failed to find any drugs.

Ernest knew the Chief would be furious. He could almost hear his boss saying, "Wait'll I get that nincompoop. Compared to what we want to find, this is small fry and could alert Carl Mingos we're on to him. Much against my better judgement, I'm forced to keep

Moneylove on this assignment. John Smith's not back yet."

Don't worry Chief. I'll get them. James never fails so neither do I. I'll get the crooks and their drug stash. Ernest was convinced there were drugs somewhere on the premises as he had noticed some quiet exchanges of nods and half smiles during the evening. He wondered why the police had not found any.

The following Saturday night Ernest was again a guest of Carl Mingos. After a short time there, Carl took Ernest's arm, and guided him to a quiet corner of the room, away from the noisy crowd.

"Tell me more about this family company you're such an important part of," Mingos asked.

Ernest began, and warmed to the subject. "My brother-in-law owns it, but I'm his right-hand man. I give him advice and have access to everything, including the keys for locking up at the end of the day. That includes the most confidential business files."

Carl smiled. "Tell your brother-in-law we would like to do business with his firm...perhaps he could take over some of my company's exports. We have not yet established ourselves fully here in Australia. For a start, perhaps you could get us information on whom your company does business with. That way we would know if we've already had dealings with them, and if so, share information with your firm...through you, of course."

Ernest assumed what he considered was a businessman's stance. His chin was raised several millimetres and he looked down from under lowered eyelids as he spoke. "No sweat, but can you give me some details on what information you might need?"

Move Over

"Of course. Come over on Tuesday morning. My secretary will have all the information on how you and I can be of great financial benefit to each other."

A girl tapped Carl on the shoulder. He nodded at Ernest and moved away.

Ernest decided to visit the toilets, in a desperate attempt to pick up something of value from any conversations he would listen in on. He entered the hall. As he passed the door to the garage it made a clicking sound. Surprised, he opened it. It looked no different than before. Fascinated by the classic design of Carl's Porsche, Ernest walked in and around the car to examine it closely. As he leaned over to peer through the driver's door, his back made contact with the wall behind him. It made a grating sound. He swung around. The wall was in panels. He watched the one he had struck fall slightly backwards. It slid behind the panel beside it. To his surprise Ernest found himself looking over a gate in a low dividing fence, and into the neighbouring Lynchs' barbecue area.

This is interesting. He walked through the gate and onto the adjoining property. A noise behind him made him freeze. Before he could turn around, something was poking into his back. He decided it must be a gun.

"Smart aren't you," spoke a voice. "Not as dumb as you look. Keep walking to the back door over there, and into the house." Ernest was happy to oblige, not wanting to anger a man with a gun.

The man kept prodding Ernest until they were inside the kitchen of the house. Carl Mingos, another man, and a woman he recognised as Liddy Lynch were standing beside a table on which containers of powder were stacked. Directly in front of him, Ernest saw that, on the floor, beside a bunched up kitchen mat, there lay four floor tiles joined together to form a square. They lay beside a hole in the floor. Several white bags, bulging with their contents, were lying beside it.

So that's where they hide the drugs. Even if the house was searched the hiding place would never be found. But where's that chubby fellow Doug who Agnes told me about? Glancing around without moving his head he saw, on a side table, a wig, a set of false teeth, and a pillow-like mound. *So Mingos and Doug Lynch are the same man. Smithy would never have worked that out. This is real James Bond stuff.*

"I found him sneaking in through the garage. Will I finish him here and dump him somewhere?"

"No, Jude," said Carl Mingos thoughtfully. "He's obviously working for the Feds so we don't want him traced back to here."

"What then?"

"We'll dump him all right, and he has to be dead when we do. I have an idea. Donny, make up a glass of very strong alcohol, and Jude, get out those sleeping tablets. They're in the top drawer of that cupboard over there."

"Good idea," voiced Donny, as he poured from a bottle into a glass, while Jude located the tablets. Mingos proceeded to hold Ernest's head firmly while they forced tablets down his throat, followed by the alcohol. Struggling did nothing to stop them. Ernest began to feel too listless to move. Satisfied, the men settled him into one of the chairs.

"What now Carl?" asked Jude.

Move Over

"I've worked it out Liddy. You'll drive him up to the lookout. It's not far. There he will fall over that steep drop near the top...an accident. He'll still be fairly coherent when you get there, so you will persuade him to get out of the car. Should other couples be anywhere around, put your arm around him. Guide him over and close against the high rail and push him. Make it look as if he leaned over too far and over-balanced. Then yell for help."

Liddy was horrified. "But that's murder. You hired me for an acting job. I want no part in murder."

"No choice. These sorts of accidents sometimes happen at lovers' parking spots. I'll wait about ten minutes before I get Anita to come for a drive with me. I'll flick the car lights as we're coming up towards you. I'll make sure we're the first; thereafter you scream that your boyfriend has fallen over the rail."

Liddy was annoyed but accepting. "Okay, but I don't like it."

"Better than jail. Come on boys, get him into the car. If anyone sees us, they'll think we're taking a drunk home. If Lorna comes over looking for him in the morning, we'll tell her he left with a woman in her car and they did not return."

The two men half dragged the muttering Ernest to the car and pushed him into it. Liddy climbed into the driver's side and started the car. Ten minutes later they were at the base of the lookout. Liddy drove very slowly. No other cars were parked in this lower section. A few metres further on she pulled up beside a narrow hikers' track that sloped gradually downward, through bushes and trees.

Liddy hurriedly got out of the car. She opened the passenger-side door. 'Come on out Ernest,' she commanded. Ernest responded by swinging his legs out the door, but he made no further effort. Liddy tugged at Ernest's clothes until he slid out and managed to stand upright. Liddy moved behind him and nudged him the few steps to the start of the track. Once there Liddy gave him a hard push. With a surprised grunt Ernest fell to the ground. In trying to get back up on his feet, he rolled over and over, down the steep grade and out of sight.

Liddy quickly climbed back into the car. "I'm no murderer, and if he does remember anything when he wakes up in the morning, we can say he was in a drunken stupor when he left the house," she muttered as the car moved forward. Higher up the hill, Liddy parked close to the safety rail Carl had referred to. She knew that, as it was not a place lovers chose to park – the view was better further up – no attention would be given to her. She stood closer to the rail.

It was only a few seconds before she saw car lights coming up the road. They flickered several times. She knew it was Carl's car, and shouted, "Help, my boyfriend has fallen over."

Carl pulled up behind her. He and Anita rushed over to Liddy. Anita put an arm around her. Some other car lights further up were now being turned on. Several people raced down towards them.

Liddy put on a weeping act, while Anita peered over the rail and called out.

Police cars arrived and almost surrounded the two cars, blocking other cars from entering. A drug squad car followed. It was forced to park further down, close to the hikers' lane entrance.

Move Over

John Smith from the drug squad slid out of the car's passenger seat, intending to walk the rest of the way up. He turned to the driver. "Did you hear something? It sounded like some drunk talking gibberish. It's coming from down that path."

"I heard it too. It's worth a look." The driver handed Smith a torch from the car.

Standing at the very start of the track Smith shone it down. It lit up a figure staggering up towards him. As it came closer, Smith recognised a swaying stumbling Ernest.

He grinned. "Well, it's my dear friend Ernest. Get lost did you, while out having a drinking session with your new girlfriend instead of catching the druggies? The Chief's not going to like it when I tell him about this. You're really going to get a piece of his mind this time.

Aren't you lucky I found you? If your friend across the road was not sticky-beaking and saw them throw you into a car, you'd most likely be dead meat by now. These people don't muck around. This Lorna woman then watched Mingos and Anita drive off in the same direction. She got so worried she called us. If not for her, you'd be wandering around here all night, keeping company with hungry mosquitos.

I always seem to have to rescue you and finish your assignment for you. I'm sure you're deeply grateful, as the Chief will be."

Ernest was now close to John Smith. "So Smithy, you've come to take credit for my work. You're not only a crawler, you're a liar, and a thief. But it's me that's nabbed Carl Mingos and his mob of druggies...just like James Bond. It's me that knows where the drugs are hidden. This time the Chief's sure to give me a raise...I think."

The self-satisfied John Smith did not understand one word of the slurred speech. He turned to his driver. "Constable, I'm going to walk up to where the action is. Give Mr Moneylove a hand before he collapses in a drunken heap."

As the constable walked down the track, Ernest raised his voice to announce to the world, "James Bond, here I come. Get ready to move over."

* * * * * * *

Why do they call it rush hour when nothing moves?

* * * * * * * *

Consciousness is the only movement.

WAITING FOR THE POSTMAN

CAN YOU BELIEVE IT?
I'M LEAVING FOR GOOD.
NO MORE WORK,
NO MORE TRAINS,
NO MORE WORRIES.

Forget newspapers; forget time,
Forget the world,
Except my bed, my house,
My garden, and my cat.
That will be my world.

Cranky bosses,
Jealous fellow workers,
Bossy junior managers,
NO MORE! NO MORE!
Freedom will be mine.

I'll have a party, two perhaps.
I'll go to lunch with all the girls.
They'll be so glad for me.
I shall take up classes,
No use being idle.

Oh the joy of new discoveries!
I'll find a profitable hobby.
I'll take up crafts,
Make presents for the kids.
Christmas will soon be here.

But my greatest joy will be,
Waiting for the postman,
To bring the news,
That I've got,
THE OLD AGE PENSION.

Vera M. Murray

WHEN YOU'RE OVER THE HILL

I had made up my mind,
I was over the hill,
And wanted no more to do,
With committees of any kind.
I'd left that all behind,
'Cos, after about an hour or so,
I'd be wishing I was out of there.

But then, to my surprise,
My friend Sandy said,
'Will you stand in for me,
At tomorrow night's meeting?'
'No, I'm past all that...too old.'
But she begged and begged,
So I weakened and agreed.

On that meeting night,
After all were seated,
I could have died,
When the secretary said,
'To keep you all up to date,
This group was created
To help save the crocks.'

She and all the other speakers,
Lost me from the start.
So it wasn't long before,
I was cat-napping.
I did try to keep alert,
But it was not only me,
Who yawned and shuffled feet.

Move Over

Business on the agenda,
Was finally all dealt with,
Agreed upon, and noted.
It seems the lucky crocks,
Will get more volunteers,
Workers, carers, visitors too,
To look out and care for them.

At last came the tea.
It was hot and very sweet.
I had two cups,
Then got up to leave.
As I shuffled to the door,
I was stopped right in my tracks.
'Wait,' said the secretary.

She was smiling sweetly.
'Thanks for coming, dear.
Perhaps we'll see you next month?'
'Hmm...No, I don't need to come,
Sandy will sure be O.K. by then,
And with your group's help,
I'm sure the crocks will also be okay.'

'Crocks? You mean CROCODILES?
Where-ever did you get that?
No, dear...ROCKS!, not crocks!
Mainly Ayres Rock dear.
You know, in Central Australia.
Tell Sandy hello for me...bye.'
She hurried quickly away.

MOVE OVER! Assignment 7
Caught Unawares

ERNEST Moneylove, being short and slim, was still desperately trying to improve his physique by attending the local gym several times a week. His unruly hair was now greased down. It caused his wide mouth to look larger and did not help his overall appearance. It fell short of being anything like James Bond in appearance. His girlfriend Estella had heard him say, many, many times, 'Move over James Bond. I'm going to be up there at the top with you shortly.' She wished he would hurry up, as she told him she could not wait forever.

On this particular morning, Ernest, his expression serious, arrived at the Drug Squad Office ready and eager to bring another drug dealer to justice – one more than his pushy fellow agent, John Smith.

He had not been seated at his desk very long, before he was called into the Chief's office. He quickly tied up a loose shoelace before scrambling hastily upright, before barging into his boss's office.

His waiting chief, Mr Grant Stand, sighed as he watched Ernest's clumsy entrance and muttered, "Why am I cursed with this bumbling daydreamer?"

"Sorry sir, I didn't hear what you said," spoke Ernest as he fronted the boss' desk.

"You weren't supposed to," snapped the Chief; his narrowed eyes staring into Ernest's.

"NO...SIR."

The boss sucked in his breath. He was silent for several moments before announcing, "I have an assignment for you Moneylove."

This one's sure to get me up there beside you James, so be ready to move over.

"MONEYLOVE...to continue....John Smith was originally assigned to this investigation. However, he phoned in this morning to tell me he's gone down with a bad case of the flu. He's confined to bed and therefore unable to travel."

What a sneak. Smithy was okay yesterday. If he's got himself out of this assignment there must be something wrong with it. I wonder what it is, but, no matter, I've got James Bond's system to follow.

"Moneylove, listen carefully. We've received information that supplies of marijuana appear to be coming from the Sunnyland fruit growing area, which is mostly scrubland. Properties there are large. Some are covered by thick growth, while others are fruit farms. Just where, and on whose property it's being grown hasn't been found. This is what you're going to find out Moneylove."

Sunnyland...the bush. I've always wanted to see the bush...now I'm goin', and it'll be like a paid holiday.

"YES SIR."

"Go now to the store downstairs and pick out a set or two of worker's clothes, and don't forget we're on a budget."

"Yes Sir."

Ernest backed to the door, bumping into it. Red faced, he turned and opened the door quickly. He was pleased he did not know what his boss was now muttering. He returned to his desk and prepared for his assignment. He grinned across at the closest fellow worker, Nigel, before entering the lift to go to the store below.

The following morning Ernest, dressed in khaki work clothes, and with a backpack slung over his shoulder, boarded the train to Sunnyland. His boss had informed him as to which carriage to board. As he climbed in, he almost tripped over an assortment of bags lying on the floor. As he tried to regain his balance the train jerked as it took off. He was pitched forward. Before he could recover, a hand shot out from a nearby seat and jerked him back upright.

He turned, to find himself looking into eyes set in the plain features of a long-haired girl in tight jeans. He noted her eyes were pools of blue...his favourite. *Not like the beauties James attracts, but one has to start somewhere, and she does have beautiful eyes.*

She jerked her thumb towards the vacant seat beside her. "Sit." It was more a command than an invitation.

Ernest obeyed. He squeezed past her and flopped into the seat beside the window.

"It's not hard to see that you're also a fruit picker going to Sunnyland."

"Yeah," he replied.

"Your build doesn't look the best for all-day physical work, and I see ya gear is new...first time?"

"Sure is...but money's scarce at the moment. One has to do something to earn a crust. What about you?"

"Been to the same place before. They feed ya well there." She stretched to make herself more comfortable, and added, "Me name's Carol."

"I'm Ernest...Ernest Moneylove."

"Really?" Carol looked amused but refrained from laughing.

Move Over

Ernest made no reply. He did not consider it necessary to admit to a stranger that he was an admirer and fan of James Bond, and his adopted name was in line with the people James met or associated with in the films that recorded his ability to succeed as a spy.

"What's the set up on the property?" he asked.

"It's a large property, like all the others around there, but half of them seem to be completely covered in bush. It doesn't seem to bother anyone. Perhaps no one lives on them. On the Bentley's property, there's a large house where the Douglas family live and at the back is a big shed attached to the house, where the fruit is sorted, packed and sent to buyers. Also, further back behind the main house is another smaller house. I believe the elderly, retired, Bentley couple, the real owners, live there. When these owners retired, they leased out their property to the Douglas family. On the right of the main house is the accommodation for the workers. We're not allowed to wander. You have to keep within the fenced boundary enclosing our quarters, when off duty, or the dogs'll tear you to bits.

They told us that some fences around the property are electric, as it was apparently a horse farm once, but no one knows for sure. It's now gone mostly back to bush, so you wouldn't want to wander too far from the farm. You'd be completely lost."

Eight hours later, the train pulled into Sunnyland station, much to Ernest's relief. He had fallen asleep several times, only to be shaken awake by Carol. She told him he was snoring. *I wonder if James snores...no...no...what am I thinking?*

After a two-hour bus trip over mostly unsealed terrain that Ernest thought would never end, they arrived at the farm late in the afternoon.

Ernest filed out of the bus with the others and followed behind Carol to stand before the overseer, a tall man, brown of face and arms from the sun. He was called Longley. He was in the company of two dogs, Gin and Tonic. *I don't recall that James ever had to deal with two, rough, savage, mixed-breed dogs like these mongrels. I'll have to make friends with them somehow if I want to search the place. Dogs love food. If I can do it without getting too much attention, I'll save some from our meals to give them. That should make them friendly towards me.*

The group followed the overseer to their living and dining quarters. At the entrance he called their names one by one. Each was given a number to match the one on their allotted sleeping area. This was followed by a late meal in the dining room. Ernest ate hastily, to be one of the first to reach his allocated bed. He was fast asleep seconds after climbing between the sheets.

The next morning Ernest and his fellow fruit pickers were each given a basket, which they were to fill. They were told that a truck would drive down later and as it drew level with each worker their basket would be emptied into it. He was pleased that he and Carol were allocated the same area.

On that first day Ernest kept up with the other pickers but it soon became apparent that he would be lagging more and more behind them as each day passed, as his back and arms ached more and more. His basket was never full when it was emptied into the back of the truck. *I'll be having a word or two with my gym master when I get home. I should be as fit as a boxer after what I pay him.*

Ernest knew he was there to investigate, and was growing impatient. He wondered how he could leave the workers' area without being seen and questioned. *I know now why Smithy didn't take this on. I bet he suddenly got better once he knew I was sent on the job, and is now back in the office. But, if I don't succeed I will be recalled and the Chief and Smithy will never let me forget it. But James Bond, always found a way, so I will too. But how can I get past the dogs? James would never be afraid of two savage dogs, and neither am I. I'll have to give them more food...from other's discarded meals when Longley's not looking. That'll make them my friends.*

Several days had passed when he was called into the home office, which was situated beneath the highset residence. *I'm getting good at this fruit picking, so they're probably going to give me a 'thank you,' or maybe a bonus for my good work.* However, Ernest possessed a small fear which had crept in. *Although unlikely, if I was sent packing I know the Chief would transfer me to desk duties where I'd die of boredom.*

On entering the office, Ernest stood stiffly, almost at attention, before a dark-haired young man and a grey-haired older man, obviously father and son. They surveyed his narrow build, before the old man beckoned Ernest to sit on one of the chairs on the opposite side of the table. The older man rubbed his hands together as he smiled at Ernest. "I'm Don Douglas, Manager, and this is my son Lenny."

"Pleased to meet you both," muttered Ernest nervously.

"You haven't done this work before have you?"

"No...no," stammered Ernest.

"We realise that. Being your first time you're not keeping up with what we expect from our workers. However, as you're probably here because you need money, we've decided to transfer you to the packing shed. It's the large shed at the back of the house. It's off limits to the fruit pickers generally, but we'll give orders that you're permitted to go there to work. You'll be escorted there and back each day by Longley and his dogs. Are you agreeable, or would you prefer to leave the farm immediately?"

My lucks in...the Bond luck has rubbed off on me.
"Well?"

"Oh yes, I'll stay...thank you sir...thank you."

"That's settled then. Off you go. Longley will bring you over in the morning."

Ernest scrambled to his feet, and backed out of the office, still muttering, "Thank you...thank you sirs." The two men raised their eyes and grimaced.

At six-thirty in the morning Ernest was ready. With the usual chop bones and pieces of discarded food stuffed into his pockets, he joined Longley, who escorted him into the shed. Ernest found it held everything necessary for sorting and packing the fruit to send on to their customers. He was allotted a place between two workers and told to copy them, as they sorted the fruit by size and colour as it moved along a conveyor belt. He noticed some of the sorted fruit was kept separate and taken into an adjoining room.

"Is that for family and friends?" queried Ernest of the nearest worker.

"Nah...some buyers only want limited amounts so they're packed separately, in that other room over there."

He nodded towards open double doors in the far wall. "They go into the same size boxes in there, but they're padded in the bottom so the fruit doesn't roll around and get bruised."

"Ahhh..." muttered Ernest as he looked around the room. He had already noticed another sorting table in this large room, and wondered why a separate room was used instead of that one. *That needs investigating...might turn up something.* He tried to think how he could get into it to check it out.

During the days that followed, Ernest, now confident he had made firm friends with Gin and Tonic, decided to sneak over at night when no one was around, to investigate further. He did not believe they would lock up the place with the dogs on guard.

Shortly after nightfall, and with the usual treats for the dogs in both pockets, he crept over to the shed. He turned the door-knob, but the door remained tightly shut. Disappointed, he skirted the shed. Checking the windows he found one to be unlocked. He had no trouble pulling it open and climbing through. He found himself in the smaller packing room. He drew out his torch and swung it around.

On a long table there were sealed fruit boxes addressed to several different groups. He took out his pad and pen and jotted them down. After closer examination of a box partly filled, he tugged at the sealed padding. It came out easily and he used his penknife to cut it open. Marijuana fell out. *Jackpot!* He shoved handfuls of it into his pockets.

Ernest froze. He could hear heavy footsteps coming from the main room. *Should have closed the window...silly me.* Before he could make any attempt at hiding, the door was flung open, and the room's main lights were switched on.

"What are you doing here?" demanded a loud voice that he recognised as Longley's.

"Well... well... looking for cash sir," stammered Ernest.

"Then what are you doing with weed spilt over the counter, and on your hands?"

"Lucky find. I won't tell. I'll keep quiet."

Longley laughed. He loudly called for Percy who came barging in.

Percy smirked. "Caught him I see. You're pretty slick. The boss'll be happy. I always thought he looked a sneaky bod."

"Gag him while I hold his arms. We can't do anything with him here, but I've got an idea."

Ernest was about to cry out but Percy was too quick with the gag so he could only murmur his protest. Tying it tightly, Percy jerked Ernest's arms back to behind his back, and tied them tightly. Pushing him roughly, Ernest was forced to march ahead of the two men, until he was jerked to a sudden stop at the side of the farm truck. With Longley's help he was thrown roughly into the back. Gin and Tonic jumped up and settled beside him. "Guard him," they were told.

The vehicle moved. Ernest's body thumped up and down on the back section of the truck as it bounced over the uneven surface of the road. They were following such a narrow track that the truck at times hit and cast aside branches of trees growing on either side. The moon had risen so in its light Ernest watched carefully to make sure he would be able to find his way out if he was dumped in the thick scrub, hopefully when still alive.

Move Over

Things worse than this have happened to James, but he kept his cool and came out victorious. So will I, but I wish my back was not lying on top of tools, especially an axe.

When the truck screeched to a halt, Ernest's head was flung against the side of a large metal toolbox. He groaned, but was ignored as the two men jumped out. They walked around to pull him roughly off the truck and drag him along the ground. They let him drop beside a circular metal plate. It was set into the loose dirt on a rise in the ground.

Ernest looked around. The full moon enabled him to see beyond the spot they were at. Through the open area, extending below them, were rows and rows of cultivated plants.

Marijuana! Jackpot! All I have to do now is get away. What would James do? I have to think. Before he could make any escape plans, Percy had tied some rope around his legs, while Longley dragged aside the round cylinder. A large gaping hole was revealed.

"Shove him down into the old well. We'll get the next orders from the boss."

"He won't last too long down there anyway," was Percy's comment.

They jerked Ernest to the edge of the hole, and shoved him almost head first into the well. Ernest closed his eyes, expecting a long fall to a far distance bottom, but he found himself in a cramped position, half sitting, half lying, upside down on a bed of damp earth. His feet almost touched the underside of the lid when they drew it back in place. He began to feel cold as the dampness of the mud soaked into his clothes. He heard a muffled voice say, "We'll come back tomorrow and finish the job."

At breakfast the next morning in the workers' dining room, Longley told the pickers and sorters that Moneylove had been sleep walking, fell, and hit his head. He claimed they had taken him to the local medical centre, and his belongings would be held in storage until he returned.

Carol could not believe Ernest would wander off without mentioning his intentions, especially with the dogs on guard. She followed Longley at a distance, so as to be unnoticed by him, as he made his way to Ernest's sleeping area. She watched him gather up Ernest's belongings and leave with them.

Waiting until Longley was out of the building, she walked over to Ernest's bed. She had seen Ernest put his mobile phone under his mattress, and the men had not looked there. She thought that perhaps he had left her a message on it. If not, she was certain she would be able to advise someone, that Ernest was in the local hospital.

She slid her hand along beneath the mattress and was pleased when her fingers closed around the phone. She opened up his list of phone numbers and dialled the first. A response came quickly. 'Nigel here...is that you Ernest?"

"No, this is Carol, a friend of Ernest's. He's disappeared. We're told he's at the local medical centre but I don't believe it. He wouldn't have gone wandering at night without him telling me about it. We heard nothing, and there're some savage dogs here that bark at anything."

'When did you last see him?"

"At tea last night."

"Okay...we'll send help...don't worry."

"Will you let his family know?"

"Sure thing...bye." She pocketed the phone and left for work.

Shortly before lunch there was the sound of a helicopter flying over. Carol was surprised and could not believe it had anything to do with Ernest's disappearance. It landed on the road not far from the farm house. Almost immediately several police cars skidded to a halt outside the main gate. Running men from the helicopter joined them.

The leader, John Smith, led the group, giving several men instructions to circle the house, and told others to circle around to the back, cutting off anyone who might decide to leave. The remaining men were to stay with him.

As John Smith had his foot on the first step of the house, Gin and Tonic raced forward. Gin gripped his leg. He had difficult holding back a cry of pain as blood spurted. Longley suddenly appeared from inside the house. Before Smith could open his mouth to shout, Longley had called the dogs off. They retreated, still snarling.

"They should be tied up. Go to it."

Longley tapped his leg and the dogs flopped on the ground beside him.

"Perhaps that can wait," continued Smith. "To get to the business on hand. This is a drug squad raid, and we're seeking one of our members. His name is Ernest Moneylove. Do you know where he is?"

Longley stiffened, but quickly recovered. "I believe he fled. The work was not to his liking it seems. As he was a lousy worker he won't be missed."

"True, but there's only one problem. He wouldn't have left without advising us, as he gives us an hour-by-hour coverage of boring information, relative or not. We've checked the medical centre. He never turned up there, so where is he? Would you like to tell us?"

"Dunno." Longley shrugged.

Smith turned to his men. "Two of you go in and search the house." Two constables disappeared inside, while another two remained with him.

A shout came from behind the second house. Smith, limping, and with his two assistants, hurried to investigate. At Smith's order, one assistant stepped behind Longley and pushed him on when he tried to stop.

They joined the constables now standing at the entrance to a car track leading into what appeared to be dense bush. The two dogs kept pace with them.

"There's fresh car tracks going straight into the bush."

Smith looked to where he was pointing and agreed. Turning his gaze towards Longley's work truck he continued. "I take it that's working.'

Longley nodded. "Then you can drive us down there and we'll see what we can find." Longley shrugged and climbed into the driver's seat. The dogs jumped onto the back.

As they moved slowly forward, Smith's two assistants kept calling out Moneylove's name. There was no answer and nothing unusual was sighted.

They eventually came to a clearing, surrounded by bush less dense than what they had already driven through.

"Stop the truck here," commanded Smith. Longley obliged and the truck came to a sudden stop. As the men were climbing out, the last one stayed where he was and kept scanning the area on all sides.

The men on the ground circled a small locked shed, situated between two tall trees. Together they kicked the door in. It revealed only tools. "You must have a good reason for keeping tools handy in the bush. Can you give us an explanation?" Smith asked Longley.

Before he could get a response, the officer still on the back of the truck spoke up loudly, "I can answer that. I can see between the trees from up here. There's rows and rows of what looks like marijuana crops. They're growing between gaps in the bush, so they wouldn't be visible from the air."

"Jackpot!" John Smith waved his clenched fists in the air, and continued. "Poor old Ernest. He's obviously not around here anywhere. We'll send in more searchers tomorrow. But, before we leave, Constable Duffield, bring over the camera."

Constable Duffield jumped from the truck. He walked around the clearing with camera in hand.

Gin and Tonic, who had been sniffing around different areas, scampered past. They began scratching on a round metal cylinder not far from the constable's feet. He could hear a sound coming from under it.

"There's something under here. I can hear a thumping sound." There was excitement in his voice.

"Probably snakes or, maybe a hare. I'd leave it alone. If you're finished we'll be out of here," was Smith's comment. He was ignored as his offsiders dragged the lid away, revealing a pair of muddy shoes with their soles facing upwards.

Smith shrugged, and walked over to look into the hole. "Well, if it isn't me mate Ernest, loafing on the job as usual. You don't seem to do anything in a proper drug squad manner." He stepped back as the two men dragged Ernest out.

As he was being pulled to his feet and the ties cut off, Ernest spat out the now loosened gag. To the annoyance of his helpers the two dogs began to jump up on him as if delighted to see him.

John Smith, stepping quickly back to be well away from the dogs, remarked, "You look handsome with all that mud over you Ernest, but you stink to high heaven. Those dogs can't just like your...err, good looks, so what am I missing?"

Ernest reached into his pockets and pulled out the now smelly chops, and squashed pieces of fat. "Only a few tasty bits in me pockets," was his reply. He pulled out the smelly mess and tossed it to the excited dogs, who began to chew hungrily on it.

"I've now seen you at your best," sarcastically spoke Smith. "Anyway, the boss'll be pleased he hasn't got to order a funeral for you...thanks to me. I don't think you really appreciate what a good friend I am to you. The boss'll show HIS appreciation. Perhaps it could be a fatter pay packet for me."

Ernest could only think. *You're always claiming credit for all my work. One day you'll meet your match. But this time, with Carol's help...nice Carol...I'll be able to get some credit. Then Smithy, you'll be more jealous than ever.'*

He allowed the disturbing thoughts to vanish as his eyes moved over the view. They alighted on the top of a distant mountain. *When I'm up there with you James, I'll sack Smithy, and without holiday pay.*

Cameras were set up so photos could be used for evidence. Ernest was called to stand near where he was found. He tried to brush the mud from his body and clothes, but most of it had dried and could not be shaken off. *James never looked like this.*

The stinking mud, together with the odour of decaying meat, caused Smith to insist that Ernest return to the house on the back of the truck with the dogs. He would be in the cabin with the driver, and with the windows closed.

At the main house Carol was waiting. Ignoring his filthy condition, she gave Ernest a slow hug. Ernest's wide mouth was smiling even more broadly when Carol gave him a second hug. As she pulled away she pushed a piece of paper into his hand.

"My phone number's on it. Ring me sometime."

"I sure will."

They left the property, with Carol waving and the others watching on, as Smith left in the helicopter and Ernest in the back of a police van.

The next morning, Ernest, clean and keen, fronted up at his work place. He had already forwarded his report to his boss by messenger, and more arrests were in the process of being carried out while the marijuana crops were being destroyed.

I know Smithy would have reported to the boss immediately he got back. I bet he limped more to get sympathy. I wouldn't put that past him to have got sick leave for the dog bite. If the boss could give out knighthoods he'd give one to Smithy. But the boss'll have Carol's report by now, and it's very favourable to me. The boss will think up something to not give me a raise, but I don't care, 'cos the raise I want is to float up to the top. Maybe James'll move aside so I can have his top spot.

On arrival Nigel greeted Ernest with a grin on his face. "You're in for a shock."

"What?" Ernest felt nervous. *Has Smithy done something even more sneaky than usual, to my detriment?* He drew his attention back to Nigel who was still speaking in a smug manner. "That's for me to know and you to find out." There was a low giggle from another staff member.

Tossing his head in the air Ernest walked away. He knocked on the Chief's office door, and entered, ready to front whatever the Chief said that he did not like, that is, if he felt confident enough.

Inside he was aghast. There was a strange man sitting in the boss' chair.

The man stood up. He waved a hand towards the chair opposite, before reseating himself. "You must be Ernest. I'm Goodberry Smartway, your new Chief."

In amazement Ernest stumbled, kicking the leg of the chair in his attempt to sit down and twisting his leg. Finally seated, and rubbing his knee, his mouth remained slightly open.

"I can see from your expression, you didn't know that Mr Grant Stand has moved on to another government position, following what seemed to be a nervous collapse. We don't know whether it's a temporary or permanent transfer."

Ernest wondered if his ordeal had somehow affected his hearing, but Mr Smartway's presence alone, made him believe it could be true. A feeling of relief and lightness crept over him. After a few moments he was relaxed enough to dare ask hopefully. "And John Smith? He's not at his desk."

"John Smith's on sick leave, recovering from a badly infected leg, caused by a dog bite I believe. He's applied for a transfer to the same section as Mr Stand has. That's being processed now. If it does, it means you'll be our top agent. I've been going through your service record and am amazed at your courage."

Ernest wanted to say that James Bond had taught him to be fearless in the face of evil, but managed to keep it to himself, feeling it could wait.

"I have also recommended a rise in your pay...not a big one...but one nevertheless."

Ernest felt faint.

"Are you all right? You seem distracted. After your ordeal, perhaps you should have a day or two off. Go now and put in a request. It'll be granted."

Ernest mumbled, "Thank you."

He managed to almost trip over his own feet as he pushed himself up out of the chair. He was still stumbling as he left his work place.

I'm going home. Won't Estella be pleased. She keeps reminding me that her patience is nearly exhausted, but I'm sure she'll be happy to have a drink with me this time, or perhaps two...not stirred, just like James Bond likes it.

A WRITER'S MEETING

I went to a new writers' group,
Hoping to get,
Help to polish up my poetry,
And head with speed,
Through the door,
Marked *Success*'.

The co-ordinator said,
"This group is like family."
And I guess it's true,
'cause the group was full,
Of characters,
I could write about,
For years.

All were female members,
Except for one lone male.
He brought beaut biscuits,
Made by his own hand,
Which were at once,
Commandeered by,
The largest lady present.

A late-comer then arrived.
Her dog was on a leash.
She let it loose,
To wander 'tween our feet,
For bits of bickie dropped,
And gobbled up real quick,
Unseen by most.

One lady past her prime,
Read a poem of lost love,

Move Over

But obviously not forgotten.
But, I missed a lot,
'Cos somewhere,
in the midst of it,
I dozed off, 'til the clapping.

One had an Irish accent,
Too thick to be,
Recognised as English.
She bored us all,
To semi-consciousness,
With what seemed reams,
Of written words galore.

She did receive a reprimand,
from the Boss himself,
Who said in soft tones,
"What excellent work,
But it could've been…umm…,
A wee bit…a lot…umm…shorter."
We all agreed with him.

One lady collared me.
She dreamed of being an actress,
But had to give that up,
'cause, being half deaf,
She couldn't hear the prompts.
Before she gave a 'demo',
I nodded and I moved away.

I don't think I'll be back,
But then I must…to find out,
How some great stories end,
Like, if Jo's 2nd moon returns,
Or is it hiding or is it lost forever?
And whether Bill's elephant,
Is bitten by the angry ant.

* * * * * * * * *
The mouse and the worm,
Eye each other on the compost.
An ant line pauses.
* * * * * * * *
Gum leaves shiver.
Black cat stalks.
Parrot squawks.
* * * * * * * *
I knew summer had arrived when I felt the
tickle of fly's legs
As they danced across my face and on my bare
arms.

THE PIN TIN

The pin tin slowly shook his head,
Towards the purple stamp pad,
Upon the office desk,
And with a rattle the pin tin said,
"My poor dear pal,
You don't look well.
In fact, in your face I can see,
Quite a purplish tinge".

The stamp pad slowly turned,
Until he faced the tin.
Ready he was to spit out ink,
Straight at the pile of pins.
The pin tin quickly acted,
Snapping shut his lid in time,
And wished within his heads,
That naught he'd said.

"I'm popular, not like you,"
Rambled on the stamp pad,
"I'm always getting patted,
By pretty office girls.
You're nothing but pricks
 That hold together dull paper.
'Till pen and paper both get pitched,
When another thumb gets pierced."

"Shut up you fool!"
Spoke up the pin tin.
"Don't talk to me like that."
The stamp pad spat back,
"Close your lid stupid,
The office girl's coming."
"I know! Why don't you cool it?"
"We pins are always cool."

The office girl glanced down,
At her desk and muttered,
"I need time off, and plenty.
I keep hearing voices,
From someone I can't see,
Who keeps moving things around."
The pin tin kept himself so very still.
The stamp pad shut his lid and slept.

* * * * * *

Thee greatest pleasure in life is doing what people say you cannot do.

HANNA'S GHOST

Hanna claimed she saw a ghost,
At night in the garden.
Her husband was suspicious,
As no amount of searching,
Found the ghost.

Hanna got more distressed,
As she continued to claim,
It came into their bedroom.
Her husband was a deep sleeper,
So he saw nothing.

Sometimes she woke, she said,
To find herself outside.
She often had leaves,
Caught in her hair.
'Sleep walking,' she lisped.
She said her nerves,
Were very much on edge.
With much persuading,
Her husband agreed,
A break away was needed.

Move Over

After months she came back,
A boy-friend in tow...and broke.
It seemed strange,
But he resembled,
Her description of the ghost.

Hanna was prepared,
To tell her husband,
She loved him still,
But she needed,
Something more.

Her husband was gone.
He'd left her a note.
"Hanna, my dear wife,
I saw your ghost.
It was a woman.

She's taking me
To her distant world,
Somewhere overseas.
I may return,
But then again...."

* * * * * * * *

Only two things are infinite, the universe and human stupidity, and I'm not sure about the former.

Printed by Libri Plureos GmbH in Hamburg, Germany